I0691416

In Cemetery Park

First Edition

Published by The Nazca Plains Corporation
Las Vegas, Nevada
2009

ISBN: 978-1-935509-56-1

Published by

The Nazca Plains Corporation ®
4640 Paradise Rd, Suite 141
Las Vegas NV 89109-8000

PUBLISHER'S NOTE
In Cemetery Park is a work of fiction created wholly by *Wade Wright's*
imagination. All characters are fictional and any resemblance to any
persons living or deceased is purely by accident. No portion of this
book reflects any real person or events.

Cover Photos
Andreas Meyer and Sophie Asselin

Art Director
Blake Stephens

Recognition

Simply, to all individuals that have lived through all of the life changing experiences of realizing that for way too long, they have been living a false life, and are now, finally, taking the moves to set things right!

And as you, the reader, might just happen be one of these people, I congratulate you for the steps and actions that you have taken. Smile with accomplishment!

In Cemetery Park

First Edition

Wade Wright

Contents

Contents continued

Chapter One

Today Sure Was One of Them!

Some days things just do not go quite right, no matter what you do. Today sure was one of them!

I closed up the garage, I'm a mechanic, at about 9:30 or quarter to ten, drove over to Shirley's — that's my girl friend, and thought we were gonna go out and get some pizza, and then, (smile on my face) —find some nice quiet safe sex place where I could take care of my twenty three year old's cravings for having some good, hot, active, wild, passionate — sex!

Well, the drive over was fine, but then without so much as a hint of trouble, we got in my Jeep and I could have sworn somebody had stolen my battery! Pretty damn embarrassing when you are an auto mechanic and your own battery goes dead on ya! Well, sad story over quickly, we ordered pizza in, sat and talked and watched some crappy stuff on TV and other than some smooching and kissing, nothing that even came close to sex since "Mommy" and "Daddy" were expected home at some time. What time, who knew, but sometime, and I'm sure they would have walked in right as I was letting out some loud "Ohs" and "Ahs" and letting the old football boy's juices come flying. Hey man, when you are used to being the high school jock, the "man of the school and the man of the town," and when every little hint that you've ever dropped, that you wanted some sex, was immediately fulfilled, to have a night like mine tonight, was not so good!

I had decided that I'd worry about the Jeep tomorrow, and I had walked over to and home from Shirley's before, and decided that since it was nice and warm outside, and it was a nice moon lit night, I'd take the walk home and try to unleash some of my built up frustrations.

Shirley's house and my apartment are about, maybe two miles apart, but if you cut through the Cemetery Park, you can save probably a half a mile or so. It's not really Cemetery Park, but it is rather a cemetery, and then separate, a park. Because of the cemetery right there, connected to the park, not many people like being in or around the park after dark. But the me — gotta remember — I'm the ole town jock, 23 years old, former football player, six foot three, two hundred and forty five pounds, oh — wait, let me explain that and say, two hundred and forty five pounds of MUSCLE! No scary old cemetery with dead bodies in it is gonna scare me!

The north and south sides of the cemetery, and the park, are the major streets. The smaller street, called Park Road, has the entrances to both the cemetery and the park, but separate drives. It's the Park Street that the normal folks like to stay away from after dark. That's the street I use to walk between my place and Shirley's.

Two thirty in the AM, nice warm night, nice moon lit night, a dark and lonely Park Road, and I'm headed down the side of this road — no sidewalks. I noticed a pair of headlights turn onto the road, and headed toward me. Now me, not exactly some little small wimpy kind of a guy, but still smart enough to know that if I get rolled by three or four thugs, I will, and can, loose my twenty or thirty bucks and some credit cards I've got on me, so being on the smarter side of real dumb, I stepped over so that the oncoming car would not see me in the bushes.

Surprise! It turned into the Park Drive and immediately turned its headlights off — and it looked like it had a bar of emergency lights on the top. A city cop car? Hey, surprise number two! Now, from behind me, coming in from the other direction is another unit, and yeah, this is a city patrol unit, but it's a patrol bike!

I'm in the bushes cause of what I thought might be some thugs coming my direction, so the patrol bike drove right by me, and past my little bushy area, and never saw me. Now the patrol bike also drove into the Park Drive and he too immediately turned his headlights off! Now I'm curious! Really curious! Or is it just plain nosey!? Two cops, one a car and one a patrol bike, turning into Park Drive this late at night and turning off their headlights right away? They gotta be after someone or something, and I'm the kinda guy that's gonna find out just what is going on.

Sneaking through the south edge of the cemetery and staying behind some of the old tall broken tombstones that seem to scare everybody so much, I managed to get up over the slight rise and watch, as I saw the first car stop, unlock the gate to the only road into the park, he drove through, the patrol bike then drove through, and then that officer got off of his bike, and relocked the gate! What? Two cops, now in a park that is locked, and with no lights on? What are they up to? This is really perking my curiosity now!

I know the park enough to know that when they move forward about maybe a hundred to a hundred and fifty feet, the road takes a big gentle turn to the right, then starts circling left around the pond until it comes back to the other side and dead ends. In other words, right in front of where I am now secretly hiding and doing my own patrol! Gotta remember, big football boy — gotta be in the know! Specially when it's this interesting! Two cops, late at night, locked parked road

— oh wait! Hey man, wait! Wonder if they're back here doing drugs? I'll bet! I'll bet they are! Good hidden place — all by themselves — the ole drug thing! Probably busted somebody earlier tonight and now they're gonna use the evidence — themselves!

I kinda squatted there between some good ole faithful tombstones and some very convenient bushes and kept an eye on both the car and the bike, till they did come all the way around to the dead end, and parked.

Both officers got out of their respective car and off of the bike, and using their flashlights, rather scanned the area as if to just be looking for anything! They didn't look like they were looking for anything in particular, just looking the place over. Maybe looking to see if anybody else was there! Me! I'm hidden! I'm in the cover of some bushes, and I'm keeping quiet! I'm gonna find out just what these two cops are up to!

The big tall black one, I'll call him Blacky since I have no idea what his name is, opened the trunk of his car, and right then I was damn sure he was gonna be grabbing the drugs that he had managed to save for himself and his buddy!

The other one, the white cop that was on the bike, took his helmet off and hung it on the handlebars of the bike, and then turned toward Blacky and said something to him. Couldn't hear it. I was too far away.

The big black cop, Blacky, didn't have anything like drugs in his hands, but as he closed the trunk lid, rather quietly, he threw what looked like a rug on the ground. The other officer, the white guy, he just stood there and did nothing, well nothing that is till the big black officer turned toward him and all of a sudden, reached out and grabbed his crotch! The big black officer grabbed the other officer's crotch, and the white guy did nothing! I saw him just kinda look up at the taller guy, and then just stood there! He just stood there —and got grabbed! The big black officer had ahold of his crotch, and the white guy didn't push him back or make him move his hand or anything! He just stood there!

My eyes were falling out! I was kinda laying there watching, and I was actually watching one officer grabbing the crotch of the other officer and I guess he was kinda feeling up the other officer! The big black officer then reached around to the backside of the white guy and grabbed onto his butt! The white guy still just stood there and let him do it! I was shocked! I'd never watched one man just grab onto another guy's crotch or ass like that — well except on the football field where it happens all the time and is expected, but not one policeman grabbing onto and feeling another policeman! If one of 'em had been a woman officer, then I'd probably say good for him, but both of these officers were obviously men! Very obviously! Men — big men! Officers! Police officers! And one guy was really grabbing onto the other guy's crotch and his ass, pulling him up real tight like, and the white policeman wasn't fighting back any!

As the white guy, just a little shorter than the big tall back officer who I'd guess stood about six foot four just stood there, all of a sudden I realized he was reaching up and starting to unbutton the big black man's shirt, and putting his hand inside and obviously feeling the big black man's chest! These two officers were making out with each other! Two officers! Two police officers, and one of 'em a bike officer — the rough and tumble kind of a guy — they were actually making out together! I had never seen two men do that to each other, well except for the times in the shower room when, especially Tommy, one of the smaller players, if you can call six foot one, smaller, would always play around and always try to 'accidentally' grab onto one of the big black player's dicks! Then it was just funning around though! Wasn't it? It was — wasn't it? Wait — that was just goofing around — right? Tommy wasn't — shit man — never really thought about that! Shit man, never thought about it, but now that I'm thinking about it, and also watching this big black guy doing it, hell man, maybe Tommy had more of a reason to be grabbing than I ever thought! Shit man, now I wonder about Tommy!

All of a sudden I realized that the big tall black officer wasn't just feeling the white guy's crotch anymore, he was actually taking the guy's pants down, and the white guy was still just kinda standing there and letting him do it! The white guy was still rubbing the big man's chest, and he was actually letting the big guy take his pants down! The big black guy got the guy's pants pulled down, and the white guy didn't have any briefs on! His bare ass was sticking out, and holy-molly — he had a ragging hardon! He was letting the big guy undress him, and he was standing there with a ragging hardon! These two officers are actually out there getting ready to have sex! Sex with each other!

I was laying there with my eyes about to fall out and my mouth hanging wide open! I knew some men had sex with each other, but I never thought police officers did! Big police officers! And one man, one hell of a big black officer, and he seemed to be the one taking charge of what was going on! I laid there and I wondered just what in the hell was gonna happen next!

All I needed to do was watch! The big black man was getting the white guy totally undressed, and low and behold, the white guy was getting everything off of the big black body too! Holy shit man — when the white guy pulled those pants down off of the big black man, I knew right then that I had never seen a bigger dick than what the white guy had ahold of and was now licking on! He was stooped down in front of the guy I called Blacky, and he was doing stuff to that man that I thought guys only did to gals! Well gals don't have dicks but he was licking on that dick and licking on what looked like a bushel basket full of nuts, and sliding his tongue up and down those big massive muscled legs like it was some doll! He was sliding his face all the way down to the guy's feet, and then licking and sliding his face all the way up till his face was buried right up in the crotch of that big black guy! That white guy was eating up that black guy! The black guy was the one that started all this, by grabbing the crotch on the white guy, and now the white guy was using the big black guy like a rag doll!

All of a sudden, the big black guy grabbed ahold of the white guy, lifted him up, and then reached over and grabbed what, to me, had looked like a rug, spread it out on the ground, and both men laid down on it.

The big black man laid with his head to the north, and the white guy laid down the opposite direction. It only took about maybe three seconds for both of those dicks to disappear into the mouth of the other guy, just as soon as they hit the mat! Neither one said anything nor told the other guy what to do, but right away, they both had a dick in their mouth! I don't think this was the first time they had done this! They acted like they knew ahead of time what to do!

I actually gasped wondering just where in the hell that white guy put all of that dick that he, so quickly and just all of a sudden went down on! I saw him open his mouth, and all of a sudden, that dick that had to be at least ten inches long, disappeared. The whole fucking thing disappeared! The big black officer did the same thing to the white guy's dick, but at least that dick didn't look like it was beyond normal human length. It looked like maybe it might have been an eight incher or maybe a little longer. It might have been bigger, but compared to that big black log, it looked littler!

These two guys, two officers, two big very well built officers were actually sucking on each other! They had the other guy's dicks in their mouths, and they were acting like they were trying to suck something out of the end of each dick! I had never seen two guys sucking on each other before, let alone one man sucking on another man! I knew they did it, but I sure as hell had never seen it done!

All of a sudden, and I do mean all of a sudden, I realized that I was laying there on my stomach, watching what was going on, and I had my hand under my crotch grabbing my own dick, and it was hard!

I had gotten a hardon watching these two officers having sex with each other! Sucking on each other! Watching that had made me get hard! All of a sudden I realized that just seeing some person naked in a picture would have probably made me get hard since I hadn't had any sex for probably three days, and my whole reason for going over to Shirley's tonight, was to get me some pussy and some ass, and thanks to one bad battery in my Jeep, that sure did not work out — so hell — no wonder I was getting hard and horny! I was needing sex, and now here I was, I was watching two men getting sex, sex with each other, and I needed sex, but that sure wasn't the kind of sex I needed, but watching them was making me hard! I was getting jealous that they were getting it, at least maybe they were getting their rocks off, and I wasn't! I was like some little kid watching his mommy and daddy doing it and having to keep quiet and real still!

The two officers laid there and sucked on the other guy's cock for probably ten or twelve minutes when all of a sudden, the big black guy swung around and threw his face up into the white guy's ass. I saw the white guy open his legs and let the big guy move right up in there and obviously eat him out! They did that for maybe three or four minutes and then again all of a sudden, nobody seemed to say anything, they switched positions and the white guy grabbed ahold of the big black man's ass, pulled his cheeks apart and threw his face right up in there and I could see him pushing his face in good and strong! Pretty soon the black man got up on his knees and let the white guy push his face up in there as hard as he could. I watched the black man throw his head up in the air and kinda howl like a coyote. All I could think of right then was this was like one animal out in the woods doing this to another animal! Damn, my dick got so fucking hard right then that I had to open my Levi's and give it some room. I never, as hell, ever thought that me watching two guys eating out each other's asses would make me get a hardon — but it had happened! It did! I was ashamed of myself, and I was glad nobody else was around there seeing me get hard, by me just watching what was going on! And I was damn glad there was nobody there that could see me jerking on it, when I gave it some room!

Again, like it was all choreographed, nothing said, the white guy laid down on his back, and the big black guy squatted his ass right down on top of the white guy's face, and obviously the white guy was laying there eating out the big black man's ass! I just laid there wondering, what would that feel like having that big muscled ass sitting on your face. I actually put my hands up to my face and pushed on both sides of my face, trying to imagine just what those muscles pushing down on my face would feel like! I guess he had to be tongue licking him, by way it looked to me! But the whole idea of having that big muscled ass sitting there, was more than I could believe!

Then again — all of a sudden, everything flipped and the white guy was sitting on the face of the black guy! Again, another big strong muscled ass sitting there on a man's face, and his mouth doing its thing, up in the other guy's asshole! Never before had I ever thought of what it'd be like to push my face up, into some big muscled guy's ass. Hey, out on the football field, things got pretty close to it a number of times, but the guy always had pants on, and not just a bare butt with the hole showing! Besides then, I never wondered just what his ass was like inside of those football jerseys, or what it'd be like putting my face up in there! Sure saw a lot of 'em in the shower rooms, and locker rooms, but never thought about wanting to see if my nose would fit up inside of that asshole!

I could not believe how the two of 'em moved around doing stuff without either man saying what he wanted to do! While the black dude was laying there and letting the white guy sit on his mouth, he was jerking on his own big stick of meat, and I swear it was bigger now, than when they first started. Laying there, letting it stick up in the air like it was, it looked like the flagpole outside of the park entrance. Just damn near that tall, and truly, almost that big around! And of course, just as stiff! Looked like a steel pipe sticking up there! Eating out that white guy's ass must have really turned on that black guy the way that pole of his stood up and got so fucking big! I mean man — a horse — a fucking horse! And the dark mahogany color of it even made it look that much more like a horse's cock too. Damn the head he had on it looked like a fucking baseball! The more I watched the more ashamed I was of myself! I was breathing like a horse in heat too, just watching those two go at each other. I had never seen two people have such hot outrageous sex before! The two men were the epitome of what every person is looking for when they have sex!

Finally the white guy did say something to the other guy, but I was still too far away to hear 'em, since they were being pretty quiet, well except for the time the big black guy howled like a coyote, but then it was still pretty soft.

The white guy moved off of the black man, and stretched out across him, and starting biting the black man's tits! Biting 'em, and I mean biting! He wasn't licking 'em, he had 'em in his teeth and he was biting on 'em! First he bit the left one, and after I did hear the black man kinda yell "Yeah man, yeah!" then the white guy moved over to the other tit and did the same over there! The big black man again kinda yelled, "Yeah man, yeah!" Gotta be honest, I'd never had my tits, either one of 'em bitten on before, but the way he obviously liked it, I decided that sometime I needed to get someone to do it to me! It had to feel good for a guy to let out like that when it's being done!

And I guess I must be missing something cause then all of a sudden, everything changed again and now the big black guy was eating the tits off of the burly white guy! And he was yelling just about the same thing! He was liking it as much as his officer buddy did! These guys were definitely into getting their tits bitten! And then, I found out that obviously the white guy liked to get his nuts bitten on, cause Mr. Blackman all of a sudden threw his head down in between the white guy's legs, and bit onto that bag of nuts like it was a big chocolate chip cookie! I mean man, I could see him actually biting down on 'em, and of course, you guessed it, the big-bagged white guy begged for, "More man, more! Bite me man — bite me!" That I heard!

Right then, my own nuts were about to bust! I grabbed 'em, not really knowing if in sympathy for the pain that I thought the white guy should be having, or because I thought my own nuts were just about to bust! Damn man, I thought I had gotten pretty hot and heavy with some of the gals that had taken me out behind their daddy's barn and made me do stuff that I never thought I'd do, but none of it measured up to this stuff! I never thought about getting my nuts chewed on like that, and I still think it should hurt like hell, but I gotta give it to that white guy — he sure did like it! Maybe he likes pain, or maybe it's just the way he and the big black guy do each other, but I gotta tell you man, it looked like a jack hammer took ahold of that bag and those nuts when the black guy took 'em into this mouth and clamped down on 'em! I guess he liked doing it and having it done, cause he then gave his own bag of nuts to the burly white guy, and got it done right back to himself! The only funny thing was though, that this time the white guy had a little trouble getting both of the big black balls in his mouth at the same time. He had to get the left one in, and then poke the right one in with his finger! Big balls! I'd heard of guys that have "Big Balls," but this time it was no joke — it was for real! From where I was at, they each looked like golf balls. I was not close. And even where I was at, you could tell they were big! Big! And me — what in the hell was I thinking when all of a sudden I wondered it I could have gotten 'em in my mouth if I had been the white guy down there! What in the hell was I thinking! I'm not supposed to be thinking about putting my nuts in some guy's mouth, let alone wondering just what it'd be like trying to get those two big nuts in my mouth! Never in my entire life have I ever thought anything so sick! Yeah, I know that other guys do it — but me!? I'm the big ole solid body former high school football star that fucks anything I want, whenever I want — well except for maybe tonight! I was really starting to worry about just where in the hell my mind was going to right then. And even more worried about my dick! It was getting so fucking hard, just thinking about, and watching what was going on, and my crazy thoughts of what if I had happened to be part of what was going on down there?! That fucker of mine was actually hurting! It had gotten that hard! And of course by this time — it was now out in the open. I had to get it out of my pants and also out of my Fruit of the Looms! It was just too fucking hard! I was always pretty proud of the size my dick gets when I'm all hot and bothered, but man, this time it was more than normal!

Laying there watching the two officers, like I was at some drive-in-movie, I could not take my eyes off of the "screen"! I'd never even watched some homo porno video, so everything I was watching here was new to me! I'd never thought about eating out some other guy's ass before, but man, I sure as hell could tell these two sure did love it! And getting your nuts chewed on like that — now I gotta admit that since I like to do some of the rougher stuff in life — just to know I can do it and then tell people I did it, maybe I needed to try getting my nuts clamped down on real hard! Yeah, right! Do it! Who in the hell am I gonna tell, that I got my nuts chewed on by some strong mouthed man? How stupid is that thought!? Stupid yeah — but I just knew inside, that I'd really like to know if I could match that big black guy and that big burly bike cop by getting chewed on like they did! And chewed on by somebody like one of them, or both of them! Ouch, oh shit man — when in the hell did I start thinking pain could maybe be part of fun sex? I could tell when I was watching both of 'em getting chewed on that it did hurt, or neither one of 'em would have let out like they each did! Maybe, just maybe it's the true way of letting some other person, some other guy, know just how much he means to you and what you will endure for him. Maybe that kind of pain ain't really pain, maybe it's more than that! Maybe that's true sharing! Sharing your body with somebody that is that true to you! Man, all of a sudden, I was starting to realize that this whole, 'out in the park, in the middle of the night, watching two of the hottest cops anywhere around take each other into their mouths and use and share each other with the other person,' was turning out to be one hell of a lot more than just watching two guys out hiding, and having sex. These two were showing me life — true life! And as I stood there — now taking every thing off and folding it neatly and placing it on a tree stump, I knew I needed to be down there, with them, and sharing part of me with them, and part of them with me. All of a sudden, I realized that of all of the sex I had had, with gals, first young girls, then the older gals, no sex had ever meant as much to me as what these two men were sharing tonight!

These two hot cops were into each other, and as I crept closer and closer, little did I realize how true that statement was.

I was definitely keeping myself under cover, but I knew that at some time, before this night was over, I was going to be face to face with these two massive hunks of meat, and I figured that if I just happened to appear, all bare and naked, how could they get too upset? They'd know for sure there was no way in hell I was gonna say anything about them doing what they were doing, if I was out here all bare assed and showing one major hardon! I needed sex, and these two guys had been showing me better, and more meaningful sex, than I had ever had, and I sure as hell was not going to let these guys get away without finding out what sex with them, or at least one of them was like! I wanted to bite some balls too, and I wanted my balls bitten and chewed! I wanted to do some tit biting and get my tits bitten too! Hey, there were two of them, maybe one man on each tit at the same time! With that thought, I knew I was ready for whatever! Sex with a man — never thought it'd ever happen to me, never thought I'd ever want to, but now, this night, I knew I needed it, and I knew who I needed it with!

I stayed in the bushes, and I kept watching! Quietly, I kept watching! But let me tell you, when I saw the big black guy reach over and grab something and then smear it on his dick, and the white guy just rather automatically lay down on his gut and then reach back with both hands and pull the cheeks of his ass apart, I knew right away that that big black guy was gonna fuck that white guy in the ass with that big black dick of his! When I realized that, I almost gave away my hiding with the gasp I let out! I thought, 'Oh my God, he is actually gonna stick that pole of his up in that guy's ass!?' I thought there is no way in hell and back that that guy can take that much dick up in his ass! I was sure as hell he was gonna scream if that big guy even started to poke it up in him. My dick was pounding like a steam locomotive! I have never thought about getting a dick or anything else put up in my ass, and now I was gonna watch a man take something about the size of a baseball bat up in his ass! I was sure there was no way in hell he was gonna be able to take it!

I stood there breathless! The white guy laid there and pulled his ass cheeks apart. The big black guy got in position right above the white guy's ass, one leg on each side of the white guy, his dick pointing up at his own face, and with his left hand, he forced it down and toward the hole he was just about to poke! His dick was so long, he had to hold himself up high enough, above his buddy and his buddy's ass, so that he could get it aimed right! He aimed it, he got the tip of it right at the hole, and then he lowered himself down, and started in.

I was shocked! The white guy just laid there and kinda said, "Yeah man, yeah! Oh Jack come on man, come on! Put it in me man — put all of it in me! Oh Jack — oh my God man it feels so fucking good! Oh Jack come on man, lay down on top of me and let me have all of it! I want all of it, I want all of it! Oh shit man, this feels so fucking good, this feels so good! Yeah man, lay there, push in on me, push in on me! Oh Jack yeah, thanks man, thanks! Oh man when I asked you out here tonight I really forgot how fucking good this feels up inside of me! Oh Jack thanks man, thanks!"

I hid there and watched in complete astonishment of how that white guy took all of that big black dick that I now knew was named Jack. I also knew that this sure was not the first time that Jack had fucked that ass. I was really wondering just how often these two got together and did this. And yeah, I wondered if the white guy ever fucked Jack in the ass too. I really wondered just what it'd look like for that white guy to be up on top of that big black guy, fucking him in the ass. All of a sudden, I guess I was wondering that kinda out of — like if maybe I was the white guy up there? I was so fucking horny and turned on, right then all I wanted to do was go over and put my face right up in Jack's ass the same way I saw those guys doing to each other earlier. Never in my entire life had I ever had thoughts anything like these thoughts, and all of a sudden, I'm wanting to push my face up in the bare assed end of one hell of a big, well built, muscled, strong black police officer! Even when I was playing football and showering all the time with the other players, never had I had feelings about a man and his body like I had right then! I was hot! I was horny! I needed sex and I saw what I wanted — two of 'em! Two big, big bodies, and two big, big dicks! Two cops — the kind of guys you are just supposed to lust over — if you're a man or a woman, and never, never get a chance at! And now here are two of 'em, both of 'em bare assed, stiff dicks sticking out, playing around and having sex with each other!

I honestly don't know if I had actually lost my mind or what, but all of a sudden, I stood up, walked out of where I was hiding, and heard Jack almost scream. "Oh my God Bill, look! Bill look!"

Now I knew Bill was the guy getting fucked in the ass, and when Jack almost screamed as he saw me walking toward 'em, Bill tried to look up and around to see what Jack had yelled about! He saw me!"

"Oh shit man, who in the hell is that!? Who are you? Where in the hell did you come from!?"

Jack quit pumping in Bill's ass, but he never pulled out! He looked at me and asked the same questions, "Who are you? Where in the hell did you come from!?"

With my own eight incher sticking out as far as it could go, and all of my bare skin showing every little pimple and mark on it, I kept walking toward the men and then finally said, "Hi!"

Both men were stunned and shocked, I know! Bill laid there with Jack still up inside of himself, and of course Jack was the man with the dick now well hidden inside of Bill's ass!

I was grabbing my dick and my bag as I finally said, "I'm Troy! I've been watching you guys ever since you got here, and men, I'm needing some sex. Guys, I've never done anything with a man before, but after watching you two, I gotta ask you to do me too! Please men, don't be mad at me. Obviously I'm not gonna be saying anything to anybody, that's why I'm all naked and letting you see that I've got one major hardon! I've got a hardon for both of you guys! I do! I'm not gonna make any trouble, believe me men, please do believe me! I just wanna do some of the stuff you guys were doing! Please men, please! Please guys, teach me some stuff! Teach me some of the stuff you guys were doing with each other!"

Still laying there with his dick up in Bill's ass, Jack looked at me and asked, "What'd you see. What'd you see?"

Standing there trying to be the big brave football player that I used to be, I looked at him and said, "Everything. I saw everything! I saw you both come through the gate and then lock it. I saw you both standing over there feeling each other up, I saw you undress each other, I saw you licking on each other and I saw you biting each other's tits and sucking on each others bags, and I saw you sucking each other before you started fucking him. Men, I've never done anything with a man before, but the way you two treat each other and you do things for each other, I really do wanna feel that kind of friendship or love or whatever it is! Please men, please don't be pissed at me, I don't mean any harm, I really don't! I was taking a shortcut home, over to Roser Street when you guys came into the park, and honestly, I thought you were probably coming in here to do some drugs or something, and I hid to watch what you were gonna do, and then I just got all caught up in watching some stuff that I'd never seen before. Please let me do something! Please men, please! I've never done anything with any guy before, but guys, both of you and both of your bodies are a real, real turn on to me! God, both of you guys are so fucking hot looking, you are! Please guys, please!"

Even though he was still laying on top of Bill, and still had his dick stuck up in him, Jack looked down at Bill and asked, "So man, what do you say? What do you think?"

Bill looked up the best he could, and said, "Well Jack — he did come out of hiding all bare and with one hell of a hardon showing — I really do think he's gotta be pretty harmless, don't you?"

Again looking down at Bill, Jack replied. "Agreed, agreed! He's got guts to do what he did! I think we oughta give him credit for that! Besides that, look at the body that guy's got on him! And, look at the dick on him! Pretty good for a white guy, don't you think? He's one hot looking guy! You know Bill, having a new guy available for both of us might not be such a bad idea! You know as well as I do how many times we've wanted to get together and fuck around and one of the wives kinda stood in the way. A new piece of hot looking muscled ass like he's showing there might just not be a bad idea! Let's let him in on the fun — okay? He looks like good meat man, some good meat! You with me man, you with me?"

"Okay man, yeah sure! What we gonna let him in on first? What's your idea??"

"Hey Bill — I think the first thing that we oughta let him do is we let him finish up on this fucking that I'm giving you! Okay? Shall we let him finish up here? I wanna watch him humping and pumping in this ass of yours! Okay?"

"Yeah Jack, yeah! I wanna see what that dick of his feels like up in my ass after you've been up in there pounding your stuff. Come on man, show our new guy what to do and get him in me. You've already got me all greased up, so I don't think he's gonna need any grease. Let him at me! I wanna see if this guy knows how to fuck or not! And if he don't — then we can give him the ole 'freshman class teaching,' of how to do some real fucking, by letting him take it up the butt, and get fucked by you and that monster of a rod you've got! Hey, if he wants to learn, then I think he oughta learn with the big man, and the big toy! If he wants to be playing with the big boys, then he needs to take the big toy! Let's do it Jack! Let's get him started Jack! Get him on my back and up in my butt!?"

Chapter Two

But, Nothing Like This!

"Oh Jack oh Jack! Please, please don't fuck me with that big thing right away — please don't! I can't take that up in my ass, I can't!"

I was freaking out when I heard Bill telling him that I needed to learn with the big guy, and with the big tool, if I wanted to play with them.

"Hey guy, hey! Don't worry man, don't worry! I'll use this thing on you when I think you're ready, and that's not right now! Come on over here and get yourself in position to poke that stiff white thing of yours up in Bill's big ole asshole here! I've got it all good and greased and opened for you, and I can tell, just by watching him laying there and kinda flipping his ass back and forth some, that hole has not had nearly as much dick up in it as it needs. It's still hungry, ain't it Bill?"

"Oh God yes man! God yes! Oh Jack, get him in me — get him in me! Soon as you pulled out, man my ass was hungry and really empty! I wanna feel that dick of his up in my chute, I do!"

Jack rather got up and out of the way, and jokingly asked, "Well guy! You've never had that boner of yours up in some other guy's chute right — but nonetheless I'm sure you kinda know where the ole hole is at — right? Poke that boner of yours in that man laying there, man — poke it man!"

And I did! I laid down on top of Bill. I aimed my cock at his hole, and I poked it in! Man, it felt kinda funny at first. Not bad — just kinda funny! I guess with all the muscles in his ass that I was laying on, and pushing on, it was a whole lot of different feelings than when I laid on Shirley or one of the other girls! His ass felt strong — really strong! Real sturdy, real strong, real solid! Truly, it did feel like I was poking it up inside of something other than somebody's body. It felt more like I was poking it in a big warm pile of warm clay or something like that! It felt fucking good — damn good! I knew right away why guys fucked other guys, and I was damn sure, that fucking this big pile of muscles had to be one hell of a lot better than fucking some little wimp of a guy, that hadn't grown up yet and gotten all full of big solid muscles! Damn, man, that ass was fucking good, and I do mean it! Damn I mean it!

I could not imagine, that less than probably thirty or forty minutes earlier, there was no way in hell that I would have thought I'd ever, in my entire life, ever be putting my dick up inside of some guy's ass, and now I was eating it up like crazy! Man, what a fucking feeling! I must have been poking this guy a hundred miles an hour! I was humping and pumping on his ass faster and harder than any pussy I had ever been in, regardless of how slutty the gal was, and yeah — I will admit my playing around has probably come pretty damn close to legally criminal. I found out early in life that handcuffs could be used, by more people, and for other reasons that what policemen use 'em for! But hey, I figured if they wanted to take care of me and use my muscled up body, and my stiff dick for something a little more than what the normal society would accept, hell man — that was between me and the gal, and I did a hell of a lot more to some of them than I even want to admit! Hey, they asked, or demanded, and with my desire to show any living thing of just how great me and this body of stone is, I'd do it! Just thank goodness no cops — like the one I was fucking right then — ever came by and saw what in the hell I was doing.

But shit man, just think about it! If I had been caught going way out of bounds with one of those pussies, and a cop like Jack or Bill here had been the cop to find us, what in the hell would he have done? Right now I don't think he'd have done shit — except for telling me that if I didn't want any trouble, then I'd better take him out behind the barn and to the same thing to him, as I was doing to her! Man, oh shit! What if that had happened! A cop that wanted to be treated rougher and more nasty than what I was doing with that gal!

What a fucking way to find out that getting really good and really rough, and really fucking around with some big muscled guy, is one hell of a lot hotter than doing the pussy thing! Man! What a way to find out! And on top of that, not just a guy, but a cop, one hell of a big muscled cop! I can hear him — the imaginary cop — yelling at me and telling me that I was gonna do stuff to him, that at first I never thought I would ever do to a man — but then after doing just a little of it — oh shit — oh shit — what a hit man! What a hit!

I was pounding the hell out of Bill's ass, just imagining what it would have been like if he and big black Jack had found me and some gal doing some really nasty stuff! And with them being the big men of authority and men standing up for the law, what if all of a sudden, they grabbed me by the arm, pulled me off to the side, and then told me that they were two cops that liked it just as rough as I obviously did — and now, I was gonna show them just how rough I could get, but this time, it was gonna be getting rough with them, both of them! And both of them, at the same time!

Oh shit man, oh shit! Just my fucking Bill as hard as I could, and then running those thoughts through my mind, was making me go fucking crazy! I liked finding these two hunks of man and muscle the way I did — but oh shit — what if they had found me instead, and what if they had laid the law on me and made me do stuff, that at first I would have sworn I'd never do, to or with anybody! Man or woman! Oh shit what a trip! What a mental trip! These guys were converting me over to a totally different kind of a guy tonight and my whole body was feeling it!

Man, my body was having feeling like it had never had before! I was feeling parts of me that I'd never felt before! Then — oh shit man — oh shit man! Oh shit! No wonder I thought my whole body was feeling it! All of a sudden, I realized that Jack had his whole face up in my ass, and he was face fucking me, just as fast as I was fucking Bill in his ass!

Jack's face and his tongue were doing just as much back in my behind, as I was doing to Bill's behind! He had his tongue up in my ass! His tongue! Nobody — nobody had ever had their face pushed up between my ass cheeks, and for God sake man — nobody for sure as hell had ever stuck their finger up in my ass — let alone their tongue! Oh man alive! Oh shit man, what a fucking good feeling man, what a fucking good feeling! I was in fucking heaven man — fucking heaven! I'd never had my ass played with like that, never! And just the idea that a man had his tongue up in my ass just made me go that much more crazy! I had been watching that great big black patrolman fucking around with Bill, when I was hiding, so that he didn't know I was watching, and now he was actually sucking on my asshole! His face and his tongue — in my asshole! I couldn't believe it, I couldn't! A man — one hell of a hot man had his face up in my ass! Never — never — never had I ever thought that someday, some man, would have his face up in there and actually be licking on my asshole!

My whole body was going into some kind of an emergency load! I don't know what else to call it, but every part of me and my insides were ringing like some big church bell! Really, I felt like they were hitting the big deep base key on the big church or old theater organ, and it was hitting every little nerve in me! Like they were leaning on it, and holding it there! Everything was feeling funny — great, but like nothing I had ever felt before! I was really having trouble getting my mind around it! I was fucking the hell out of one cop, and getting tongue fucked in my ass by the other big cop — the great big black cop!

I was grabbing onto Bill like I was gonna fall out of him, and hell man — there was no fucking way that was ever gonna happen! Bill's ass was grabbing onto my dick tight enough to keep me from falling off of the side of a fucking mountain cliff. It felt like the sides of Bill's ass had vice grips in it, hanging on to me, and then Jack was pushing on my ass so fucking strong, that I thought Bill was gonna need to tell him to back off, cause there was too much pressure down on him!

Yeah right!! Yeah right!! There were two of us really begging for more and more! For Bill, it was more and more of my dick up in him, and pounding on him harder and harder if possible, and once I realized that I actually had big Jack's face up in my ass, sucking on my ass and licking with his tongue, I damn near went crazy myself.

When I started yelling, "Yeah man, yeah! Do it to me man — do it! Do me — do me! Deeper man deeper!" Bill tried to ask what in the hell I was yelling about, but he really had trouble trying to get the words out, since I was knocking the air out of him every time I slammed back into his butt! I finally realized what he was trying to ask and I told him that he was really getting fucked by two guys now, cause big black Jack was fucking me in my ass with his face and his tongue, while I was fucking him in his ass with my dick!

"Oh man, oh man! Oh guys — do me — do me! Oh fuck!" Then he tried to tell Jack something like, "Oh Jack, we've wanted this for years man — years! Oh shit man — Jack, we're finally getting it man! We're getting it like we wanted! We finally found our man Jack! We finally found our man!"

I had to be out of my mind, I did! Everything was so fucking good and feeling so fucking good, I was feeling like I really did not know for sure of just what I was doing! My mind was going places like it had never done before! Good places — really good places!

I kinda came to, and I realized that all of a sudden Jack had taken his face out of my ass, and I tried to look back and ask what he was doing and why did he quit, but then he just patted me on my butt and said, "Fuck him man! Fuck him! He likes your dick up in there man! Fuck him and fuck him hard! Go to it boy, go to it!"

Holy shit man, holy shit! All of a sudden, while I was fucking the hell out of that piece of muscled steel butt that Bill called his ass, I pulled up and then pushed down in — and then all of a sudden, when I came back up — I got fucked! FUCKED!! I was getting fucked, and I was getting fucked by the big black cop and his big black cock! He had actually opened up my ass and he had put his big black dick up in me! He had it up and inside of me!

"Keep it up man, keep it up!!! Fuck him man, fuck him!! Troy ole man — fuck him! He needs that dick of yours up in there — fuck him hard man — fuck him hard!!!"

Jack was actually screaming into my ear, and believe it or not — yes, he was fucking me too! Yes — he was fucking me and he was fucking me hard, and in the ass! He had taken that enormous big black tree trunk of his and he had actually put it up in my butt, and he was using all of it in me — all of it! He had pushed his big enormous rod up and into my ass while I was fucking the hell out of Bill, and when I pulled up out of Bill some, that was when he poked his enormous big rod up into me — and then when I went down into Bill to feel his insides as much and as deep as I could, that's when Jack kinda pulled out some — and then — in and out — and in and out! I was getting fucked in the ass for the very first time, while I was fucking another guy! During my very first fucking of some guy, — and I was getting it in my ass with the biggest fucking dick hanging on any guy possible!

I let out an, "Oh my God man, — oh my God Bill! Bill, he's fucking me with that enormous dick of his! He's got that great big rod of his up in my ass! Bill he's fucking me while I'm fucking you!"

Trying to look around some, all I could hear Bill trying to say was, "Holy shit man! Holy shit! He is!!?? He's fucking you? He's fucking your ass? Oh my God man, I can't believe it man, I can't! Oh Troy — Troy right? Troy he can't really be fucking you — not really! Troy, if a guy's never been fucked in the ass before, he can't get fucked by that guy and that dick of his! Maybe he's just finger fucking you and you think it's his dick! It's gotta be!"

As he was pounding up and down in me, and going for all the gusto that he could, Jack proudly stated, "Hell no man! This ain't no fucking finger I got up in there man — no fucking finger! I am fucking this guy with my dick! The same one that got measured longer than eleven inches, and more than six and a half inches around — and I'm using it on this nice new ass! Bill, like you said man — we definitely found our man! He's taking this dick deeper and harder than you do, and in about one minute we're gonna find out just how much room there really is up in that hole, cause in just about a minute or so, he is gonna get bred with some of the hottest black man cum that has ever shot out of a dick! Oh shit man — oh shit! Oh man — hold on boy — hold on — oh shit man — here it comes — here it comes! I'm coming man, I'm coming! Oh shit man, oh shit! Shit man what a fucking feeling, what a fucking feeling! Oh man, you just got one hell of an ass full man, one hell of an asshole full! Oh God, oh man — I just came man — I just came! Oh shit did that feel good, damn man — that felt good!"

Right as Jack let loose of what actually felt like about a quart of hot smooth cum — right up into my ass, the same thing happened to me, and I let everything fly right up and into Bill's sweet tight ass! All of a sudden both of us were yelling that we were cummmin — we were cummmmmin! Two guys, both at the same time were shooting our loads and being more than quiet, that we were both cummmming!

Jack collapsed down on top of me, and I collapsed down on top of Bill, and actually Bill was the only one that had enough breath available to even say anything!

"Oh shit men, oh shit! Oh God men, what a trip! Oh guys, I've never been fucked like that in my entire life! Oh men, I can't believe it, I can't! Two of you big muscled guys up on top of me, and both of you two shooting all your sweet cum at the same time! I know you're not gonna believe this, but really, I could feel both of you guys when you each shot off! Yeah, I know I had to feel you loading me up Troy, but Jack, right now I feel like you shot all of your cream right through Troy and into my ass too! I could feel you shooting man, I could! I know — how in the hell could I feel that with Troy in between us — I don't know — but I did! Man, oh man! What a trip men, what a trip! Hell guys! I haven't even shot off yet, and right now I feel like I've been shooting off for the last ten minutes or so!"

I just laid there, feeling all of Bill and his muscles under me, and then feeling all of big Jack and all of his big muscled body on top of me, and yeah, about five pounds of it up in my ass! It felt so fucking good up in there. Never in my entire life did I ever think I could have good deep feelings toward another guy, and all of a sudden, I was really feeling a lot of love with these two, hot, muscled patrolmen, and yeah — married patrolmen! I was so fucking jealous of their wives, I was! I knew they were married because I remembered hearing 'em both earlier talking about not being able to get together cause one of the wives always kinda stood in the way!

I really wanted to take both of these hunks home with me, and let them at me every morning, noon, and night! Damn that dick of Jack's up in my ass cannot be replaced with anything, and yes, that includes sex with women, any woman, and yes — Shirley included! All of a sudden, I think I knew, internally anyway, I really, truly knew I was into guy sex — anyway — anytime, and all of the time! God man! I simply knew there was nothing that can replace this! Nothing!

Jack started to pull out of my butt and I almost screamed at him to, "Keep it in me man — keep it in me! Push it in me Jack, push it in me!"

Oh man I did not want him pulling that beef steak out of my ass! I never in the world, ever felt anything that felt as great as having that great big piece of meat stuck up inside of me! Just the idea of him getting up and off of me and taking that thing out of me was unthinkable! I don't know how in the hell I ever thought I was gonna be able to always have it up in me, but damn man, I did not want him to pull it out!

"Hey guys." Jack interjected. "Guys I gotta get going! Barbara Ann's gonna wonder just where in the hell I'm at if I don't get going pretty soon. Troy my man, I gotta take this thing out of your butt, and when I do I suggest that you go over there somewhere and squat down, and try to take a shit. I know damn well that I pumped so much fucking cum up in that hole of yours that if you try and get dressed, you are gonna have a whole lot of cop cum, flowing back out of that backside."

Jack did roll off of my butt, and yes, I wanted to cry when I felt the end of that dick come out of my ass! I wanted him up and in me so bad!

Bill kinda looked back and up at me, and asked, "Uhhhh man, you gonna pull out back there, or am I gonna have you plugged into me all day?"

I was still laying there, as Bill said, still plugged into him, and I watched as big Jack got up and grabbed some rags he had in the trunk of the cruiser, and started to wipe himself up some and kinda clean off some of the grease that he had, without me knowing it, put on his dick while I thought he was just fucking my ass with his face.

I looked at him, and that dick and finally managed to say, "Shit man, how in the hell did you ever get that fucking thing up in me? That is so fucking big! Honestly Jack, how in the hell did you do it?"

Looking over at me, and Bill too, since I still had not "unplugged" from his tight hot ass, Jack said. "Troy my man, you were so into fucking that ass you are still in, that I knew you really did not know for sure of everything else that was going on around you, and after I started tongue fucking your ass, and I had your mind so out in outer space someplace, I grabbed some grease on my fingers, and yes, I started finger fucking you, but you were so fucking far out of reality, you did not know it! I got about three fingers up in there once, and that was when I decided that you were the kind of a guy that could take anything up in that hole of yours, and all of a sudden, I proved it! One aim, one push, and I had my dick up in that hole of yours! You are the very first guy that I have really been able to do that to without him screaming for at least for a second or two. Seriously man, your mind was so far out and away, I really do think I could have fisted you and you wouldn't have known for sure just what was happening back there! I just got my little ole dick all good and greasy and slam — bang — I was up in there and doing my thing!"

The more I listened to Jack telling me how he got all of that tree trunk stuck up in me, the hotter I got all over again. I was still in Bill's ass, and I was right back at pounding on it like I had never stopped!

"Oh shit man! Troy, you gonna fuck me all night long, or are we gonna call it a night pretty soon?"

"Hey Bill, I gotta cum again, I gotta! Let me fuck you till I cum again man, I gotta!"

And then I kept it up! I guess I really didn't give Bill much choice if he was gonna get fucked some more or not! I was fucking, and I was fucking like hell! I sure as hell guess maybe he didn't care, since he just laid there and let me use him and his ass for as long as I wanted.

By this time, Jack had managed to get fully dressed, and standing there, he looked down at Bill and me and said, "Hey men, I need to put that mat back in the cruiser, and I kinda guess maybe you two are gonna keep it up and going for a while — right?"

Just as Jack was talking to us, Bill almost kinda let out a low scream and said, "Oh Jack wait man — wait! Hey Jack, Troy's just about to feed me some more hot juices — I can feel it man — yeah, oh I can feel it, oh man, oh man I'm getting it, I'm getting it! Oh shit man! Oh God Troy — you did it man, you did it! Oh shit man, you shot off in my ass like a fucking cannon man, it felt like a fucking cannon, or a full force fire hose hitting me!"

I was totally speechless, I could not say a thing! Thank goodness Bill could tell I was right at the edge of one major climax, cause right then, I couldn't tell either one of the guys anything! All I wanted to do was yell, "I'm cummming men — I'm cummming guy!"

Standing there, fully attired as a very proper good-looking police officer, Jack looked down at us again and asked, "So, tell me men. You guys gonna do this all night long? I gotta go men, I gotta go!"

Bill looked up at me and asked, "You kinda done man, you kinda done? We need to get up so Jack can put the mat back in the cruiser, and I guess maybe we need to kinda call it quits for the night, don't you think?"

I finally got my breath back kinda enough to talk, and I finally asked, "Hey man. Hey Bill if I go over there and lay on the grass, will you fuck me please! Please man, please! I wanna feel your dick up in me, and besides me and big Jack over here have probably shot off at least twice each, and I don't think you have at all, even once. You been laying there on your dick and not even been able to jerk on it any! Please, please will you fuck me and yeah — yeah, mix your cum with big Jack's cum! I wanna know I've got some from both of you guys up in there before I squat and try to dump some of it! Please Bill — please!"

Looking up toward Jack, Bill said, "Hey guy! Jack I guess maybe I've got me one piece of Angus Beef here that just ain't gonna stop. We'll get off of the mat so you can throw it in the car, and I guess maybe man, I'm gonna be fucking that hot little ass you got all opened up tonight! He wants to take home some of me up in that ass too I guess, so Troy ole man, get up so we can let Jack take the mat, it belongs in the cruiser, and we'll go over here and then, I guess, I'll fuck you till the sun comes up if that's what you want!"

Bill and I did finally get up and off of the mat, and I had one fucking hardon just standing there, but I was not embarrassed at all like I would have been earlier! I kept grabbing at the front of Jack's pants and I kept asking him when were we gonna be able to get together again and let me feel him stuffing that great big thing back up in my ass. He quickly wrote down, on a card of some kind, my name and my phone number and promised me that he would call, or maybe even stop by the garage that I kinda owned — well me and more like the bank. Oh shit man, just the idea of him stopping by the garage turned me on! Without even knowing for sure if it would ever happen, just the idea of me looking up, and seeing him and that magnificent body come walking in and toward me just about made me cum without even touching my dick! I begged him to do it, "Please do it! Come see me, please!"

As I stood there, hardon and all, Jack and Bill kinda decided just how things were gonna work out, like Jack was gonna unlock the park gate, but then leave it unlocked, and when Bill left, if he ever did that night, he could re-lock it. Jack left behind some grease and some paper towels that he had brought along, and finally got in his cruiser and told us to have fun, as he then drove away.

Bill looked at me and said, "Okay man, it's you and me now, it's just you and me! I'm gonna take that ass of yours, I am! Ever since I saw you walking out of the bushes and letting us see you were here, I've wanted to see just how that ass will feel on my dick, and at first I sure as hell never thought I'd get it tonight, but man, knowing that you just got the fuck, fucked out of you by Jack and that fucking big thing he's got — I know damn well what I'm gonna get to do back there! I gotta ask you though man — are you telling us the truth when you say you've never been with a man before, and you've really never had that ass fucked? You serious?"

"Serious as all get out man, fucking serious! Bill, I've never done anything with a man before tonight! I was the guy in town that all the gals had to be able to tell all their friends the next morning that I had fucked 'em the night before! I was like the trophy of the town. Seriously man, I could have, and a couple of times, did have more than one girl in one day! But let me tell you man, doing three or four girls in one day sure as hell does not beat fucking you! Bill, there is no way in hell I can even try to tell you what it feels like to lay down on you and then put my dick up in that tight ass of yours! Seriously man, why in the hell do men fuck women when something like you is out there getting fucked! Man, I damn near went totally out of my mind fucking you and that ass of yours!"

"Well Troy my man, I gotta believe that! Seriously man, do you realize yet that you got fucked by Jack tonight? You took a tool up in you that took me about three good hot sessions to finally take all the way! Troy, that's why I asked you if you were being honest when you said you had never been played with before! Lay down there man, I may not be as big and as long and as thick as big ole Jack's, but I do know how to fuck a good looking ass, and Troy, you've got it man — you've got it!"

31

"Hey Bill, you say it ain't as big as Jack's, which is probably true, but how big is yours? I really hadn't seen it hardly any at all since you were laying on it when I came out of the bushes, and have been ever since, but shit man, look at it! It's big too! How big is that thing?"

"I measured it once, right after Jack and I did our thing together for the first time, and then it measure right at nine inches long, or maybe a little longer, and it was right at about five inches around! See Jack's is more like eleven inches long, and more like six and a half around, so you know damn well, he's got a biggie! One hell of a biggie! And, we didn't do any of that tonight, since things got kinda changed once you showed up, but just you wait till the day when you put that thing down in you mouth and then try to breath with that much meat down in there!"

As I was laying down in a nice grassy spot, and Bill was getting all grease up to put his own biggie up in me, he was talking about taking Jack's dick down in his throat and I gotta admit, that was something that I had not had time to even ponder yet!"

All of a sudden, I flipped over, looked up at Bill and almost screamed out, "Oh my God man, oh shit, do you suck on that dick!? Bill, are you telling me that you suck on Jack's dick!?"

"Oh hell yeah man, hell yeah! Gotta admit, took me some time to finally do it, but he kept sucking on mine, and I finally decided that I just had to pay him back, and so I finally got up the nerve to put it in my mouth! Well, the first time, probably only about three or four inches of it. But, over time and with practice — he now says that I'm his best cock sucker he's got."

Bill kinda took ahold of my shoulder and rolled me back over, and I could feel the tip of his cock hitting my ass when I asked him, "You're the best sucker he's got? He gets sucked off by other guys too?"

"Oh hell yes man, hell yes! Troy, when a guy looks like that man does, and if he's horny and thinks he can get away with it, he'll let that slonger hang down inside of his pant's leg and if he's really wanting some action, he'll find him some guy, driving all alone, and he'll find some reason, some kinda fake reason, to pull the guy over. And while he's standing there at the driver's window, he kinda lets it all show — a lot, and if that guy looks at it, then Jack manages to kinda rub it, and he lets the guy know he's interested. Part of the time, he actually stands there and gets a hardon — in his pants! Well you can imagine what that looks like, specially to some guy sitting right there, right beside it, in his car. If the guy is really acting like he's really curious about it, Jack'll actually ask the guy if he wants to see it, and if he gets the right answer, then Jack says, "Well guy, tell you what. If you wanna follow me over into the old wooded area of the Old Town Park, if you treat me just right, then maybe I could forget all about this ticket and just let you go. He gets a lot of action that way. Not too legal, but hey, he gets a lot of action. Men, straight men and gay men all want to see just what in the hell he is hanging in there when he's got it hanging down loose! Hey Troy, I gotta admit, that's kinda the way he and I first kinda got to know each other, in what I'd call an, 'Up and close way!' It was hanging down his leg one day when he got back to the station, and he thought he could get into the men's room and tuck it back in, but I came around the corner, and I saw it! I of course, did just like everybody else does — I looked down at it! He knew I had seen it, I looked straight at it! He headed for the men's room and I followed. I got real honest and told him, 'I don't think I believe it man — I don't think I believe what I just saw! Show it to me and let me see it!' So he did! That was the first time that I had ever touched some other man's cock! I could not resist! I just had to feel it and see what it felt like. The rest is history. He liked me feeling it, and later that night, we snuck off by ourselves and even though I did not try to suck on it that night, I sure as hell did fuck him! He told me that he didn't get many chances to get fucked, and he liked to get fucked, so that's how we started. I had never fucked a guy before, and I found out I liked it — I liked it a lot, so we started doing it about once a month. It took me some time before I let him aim that big thing at my ass, but

I finally did, and then we started playing around a whole lot more! I was just like you — I needed it! And once I got it, I needed it a lot!"

As I laid there and listened to Bill tell me about how he and Jack first started, he was poking his own big rod into my ass, and I was really starting to go back into my own little world again. I guess Bill knew it, cause he stopped talking and he started fucking like a lion! Well hell, of course I've never been fucked by a lion, but feeling all of the strong and solid muscles up on top of me, I was sure that was what getting fucked by a lion would feel like. I actually laid there, closed my eyes, felt Bill's big stiff dick going in and out of me, and I actually, sick — I know, but I actually imagined one hell of a big strong lion having me trapped down, and fucking the hell out of me! I loved it, I did! Never had I ever been so controlled and trapped down and used like I was being used right then, and I loved it! Of all of the times that I had gotten rough with some of the gals that I'd had, well sex — if that's what you wanna call it, and of all of the times on the football field, when I actually had three or four guys all piled on top of me, never had I ever had the feelings I had that night, right then.

I was a twenty two year old "kid." Yeah in my mind that night, I was a kid! No longer the "big boy on campus" so to say! I was a "kid," a guy that was being controlled by a much stronger man — a man that I guessed to be probably about thirty three or thirty four, and a man carrying around about two hundred and thirty pounds of muscle that really did make my two-forty look like soft meatloaf! All of a sudden I realized that these two guys tonight, the two that had fucked the hell out of me and my ass, were really the 'men of the town,' the 'true men' of the town! One hell of a hot muscled white guy that had the nicest trail of fur running down his chest, right in between two of the most gorgeous chest muscles that a man could have, and supporting the tits that had been chewed on really rough earlier in the night, and then — the big, big black man that every man, woman, and child had to admire, since he really did look like a picture out of a Mr. Top of the World Bodybuilder magazine or paper or something. Just anything that showed the biggest and the best of the lot. And I'm not talking about just his dick, I'm talking about all of him, all of him!

As I was laying there getting the pounding hell fucked out of me, all of a sudden I just felt like I really did need to know a whole lot more about the two men that had just changed my life! Stupid as it may sound, I kinda tried to look up at Bill and ask, "Bill how old are you? How old are you?"

Fucking my ass like a jackhammer gone wild, Bill stopped and look down at me and asked, "What!? What did you just say?"

My answer, yeah, my answer was — "Bill I love this, I love this! Bill how old are you, please tell me man, how old are you?"

"What in the hell do you need to know that for man, what in the hell do you need to know that for — especially when I'm fucking the hell out of you and your ass!?"

"Bill, I just gotta feel like I know you better than I do! Please Bill tell me about you! Tell me how old you are and if you have any kids and that kind of stuff! Please!"

"If you gotta know man — I'm forty-six and I've got three kids, two boys and a girl. Now you happy man, you happy!?"

"Bill there's no way in hell that you're forty-six man — no way in hell! Hell man, you can't be more than maybe thirty five at the fucking most man, you ain't that old!"

"What's the matter man? You having a problem of getting fucked by some older guy? Am I too fucking old to be fucking you and this tight little ass of yours? Is that what you're saying man, is that what you are saying?"

"No, shit no man! No! But Bill, you can't be that old! For God's sake man, look at you, look at you! You can't be that old man, you can't be!"

"Well accept it or not, I am. If you've got a good body man, and you take care of yourself man, you can stay young for a hell of a long time."

I don't know if Bill decided that he needed to prove what he was saying about taking care of yourself, but all of a sudden, I thought I had a steamroller working on my butt! He was fucking the hell out of me and pounding the hell out of my ass! Shit man, he was fucking the hell out of me, but I sure as hell was not gonna tell him to stop. God it felt good!

Once again, as stupid as it could be, all I could think about right then was asking, "Well how old is Jack? Bill, how old is Jack!?"

I got a reply — a real reply! "For God sake man — you wanna get fucked or you wanna talk! Jack is the one that is thirty-five. And yes, he is married and yes he has two kids, and no — neither one of our wives know we fuck around with guys, and yes — you've got one hell of a hot ass to be fucking, so now shut the hell up and let me fuck you! Okay!? Okay!?"

Man, let me tell you I shut the hell up! I laid there and I let the man do his thing, and I loved every fucking second of it, and every inch of it!

He grabbed me up under the arm pits, threw his hands up and behind my neck, and with a full nelson body lock, he had total control of me, the man and the ass that he was fucking! He was beating the hell out of my ass, and I sure as hell was gonna keep my mouth shut, cause I wanted to feel him tighten up and start shooting his juices up in my ass! I was in heaven man, true heaven!

And then it hit! All of a sudden I felt Bill's body get real stiff and rigid, and he quit pumping up and down in my ass, and for a second there, I truly thought he was trying to push my whole body down in the ground. He pushed in on my ass harder that any feelings I'd ever had before, even in football! I felt like an eighteen-wheeler was trying to drive up in me! He let out a big long string of, "I'm cummming man — I'm cummming man! I'm cummming! I'm loading your ass man, I'm loading your ass!"

He laid his head down beside me and truly, I don't know if he knew he was saying anything or not, but he kept telling me, "I love you man, I love you! You feel so good to me — you do! I love your ass man — I love your ass! I gotta eat your ass out sometime man — I gotta eat it out! Oh shit man, you are so fucking hot man — you are so fucking hot! I gotta use you a lot man — I gotta use you and I gotta use this ass! This is the hottest ass in town! Oh man, I shot you so fucking full of some old man's cum — I did! I did! Now you've got some of Jack's juices up in you, and now you've got some of mine! Squeeze your ass man, squeeze your ass and mix 'em up in there, mix 'em up! You've been fucked my some of the city's finest tonight man, some of the finest! And when I tell you the city's finest, I do mean some of the finest fuckers in town! Man, oh man! What an ass, what an ass! Come on guy. Get up, wipe some of that cum and grease out of your ass end and go get your clothes. I gotta get out of here too, or my wife is gonna be out looking for me, and right now, the very last thing I want to have happen is to have something come up that would stop you and me of getting together again. Troy, Jack is one hell of a great fuck, and a great fucker, but man I am glad, really glad that we finally found ourselves a third person. And what a person! What an ass! You do want to get together with us, or at least me, again don't you? I hope like hell you do! Shit I hope you do!"

"Hell yes man, hell yes! Bill, I never, ever thought that I'd be having sex with some guy, but shit man, this is what I call true sex! You and Jack are both such hot guys and man, I love getting fucked by both of you guys. I like sex stuff rough, and you guys can do it rough!

I watched you guys biting on each other's tits earlier, and that made me get a hardon, it did. I want you guys to bite on my tits too! I wanna see what that feels like, I do!"

"You know Troy, we don't have time tonight, I gotta get going, but we gotta get together real soon, and I'll be more than glad to bite on those tits, and I wanna taste that nice stiff dick you've got there, and, of course — I'm hoping you wanna taste mine. Hey, maybe Jack's too. Wanna do that?"

"Oh hell yes man, hell yes! This whole thing has got me so fucking turned on to doing anything you guys want me to do, I'll do anything, I'm sure just about anything! I know it's gonna take some time and some training, but yeah man, yeah, I wanna be your cock sucker and I wanna be Jack's cock sucker too!"

As both men stood there and attempted to accept the new friendship in a new and rather unusual way, checking each other out and looking each other all over, Troy then scooted up the incline and retrieved his clothes. As he got back to where Bill was now getting re-attired — hot cop pants, tight ass hugging, crotch hugging and dick showing cop pants and one hell of a tight hot bicep hugging shirt, Bill handed him a card with his name and phone number on it.

"Hey guy, here's my private cell number and I wanna hear from you, understand?"

Troy took the card in his hand, as he did so, he then reminded Bill that he had told him and Jack where his shop was at, and how he really did want both of 'em to come by and stay in touch. Then all of a sudden, as he read the name on the card, he asked, "Bill Scott? Your last name is Scott?"

As Bill looked at him he said, "Yeah! Yeah, why?"

Troy looked at Bill and rather calmly asked, "Hey guy, you got a son they call Scotty Scott? Played football over at West Side a few years ago?"

"Yeah, yeah! That's Bradley, my oldest son. Why? Why, you know him? You know Scotty?"

"Oh yeah man, oh yeah! And he knows me too! We played ball together. Hey man — we've shared some gals together too, and yeah — yeah, we've showered together too! You seen that dick on that son of yours lately?"

Chapter Three

My Hands Are Dirty!

It was Friday morning, three days after my life changing experiences, and I had my head stuck under the hood of old man Jamison's old '84 Merc., trying to once again, get it to run nice and smooth. Sometimes, trying to help out some of the old ones with their money, and not doing stuff to their cars that it really needs, just does not turn out to be the best for me — for the old man — or the car! Total tune up this time, and yeah, I admit it, I don't wanna tell him how much the total cost is gonna be, even though I am the one getting paid.

Anyway, I had my head stuck under the hood and I heard someone asking, "Troy? Troy?"

I kinda pulled out from under the hood, and damn near fainted! There he was — the most beautiful, gorgeous hunk of a cop on this side of the world! Hey, at night, out in the middle of a park, looking at stuff and doing stuff that I'd never done before, I guess I really had not seen the true 'everything' about this big man that I had my first gay sex with. Right there, about five feet away from me was Jack! The big black cop, and oh man — did he look hotter to me right then than he did the night he pushed that enormous big rod of his up in my ass, and loaded me with about a quart of some of the nicest, city employed juices, that any city employee could make, shake up, and then shoot out of the end of his dick, at about a hundred miles an hour! Oh my God, there he was!

When I heard someone asking, "Troy? Troy?" I turned my head to the left to see who was asking, and then whapped the hell out of my head when I jerked up when I, just kinda, saw the most beautiful sight that had ever been in my shop. Three days earlier and I had thought I was the "god of the world" to all the girls and horny babes around town, and now — all of a sudden, one sight of this bronze statue standing there, and I was a fucking pile of butter!

"Jack, Jack! Hi guy, hi! Man alive — I sure am glad to see you, I am! Damn man, I gotta tell you, I really didn't think I'd ever see you in here, but hey — Hi guy, Hi!"

"Troy — why didn't you think you'd ever see me in here? Why?"

"Oh Jack, Jack, seriously man, seriously man, I guess I kinda just figured that the other night was just kind of a dream to me and that was something that I was gonna have to forget about. Seriously man, I really never thought I'd ever get to see you again. I didn't!"

Looking around some, as if kinda checking the place out some, Jack then asked, "Hey Troy, you working here alone? Is it just you and me?"

"Oh yeah Jack, yeah. I sent Jimmy, he's my helper — I sent him over to Nappa, and so right now it's just you and me. Why? Why?"

"Oh just not wanting to say or do anything that somebody else don't need to see or know about, that's all."

"Uh Jack, uh Jack, what do mean? What?"

And as I asked, I sure as hell did not need any answer! The answer was grabbing onto my crotch! I damn near fainted when I realized this unbelievable hunk of a man, fully dressed in his hot ass hugging, and crotch hugging officer pants and his shirt that almost looked like it was painted on all of those muscles, was actually standing there — in my shop, and feeling my now ragging hardon. Me, just me, and I actually had one of the hottest fucking cops anywhere around, for miles and miles, and probably states and states actually standing there and rubbing my dick! He was actually in my shop and almost jacking me off while I still had pants on!"

"Oh Jack, oh Jack! Jack wait man, wait! Jack I can't touch you, my hands are dirty man, my hands are dirty! Oh Jack wait! Hey man, let me go wash my hands some, please Jack — I gotta go wash my hands!"

I turned and headed for the men's room and grabbed the degreaser, used it, washed my hands with some soap and then the degreaser all over again, and then the soap again! I wanted my hands good and clean — cause of what was already happening, and I sure as hell knew just where in the hell I wanted to put my hands, and I sure did not think that having one big greasy handprint showing on the crotch of those tight pants was gonna be a good thing. Light tan fabric and a dark black handprint of grease, sure would not go together too damn well.

"Hey guy, how long you figure till your Jimmy guy gets back? How long till be shows up?"

Just as I heard Jack asking about Jimmy, and I finished my third hand drying wipe, I started to say, "Probably about twenty minutes," and I turned around to find out that my man — my Jack, was standing there with about eight inches of his dick standing straight out of the front of his pants!

When I saw that, I flipped my head around toward the office door and then finally and calmly realized that my man, Jack, had been careful enough to keep himself over and out of the view of any potential visitors that just might happen to come walking in. He was over, kinda of behind a wall, and also well hidden behind the old Ford pick-up that I was still, someday, hoping to kinda rebuild and get into some fashion as a truck, again.

I took one look around, knew everything was safe and okay, and it only took me about one second to have my hands on that thing and start making it show all of the proud stance that I knew it could damn well do!

"Oh shit Jack — oh shit! I cannot believe this man, I cannot! Oh my god man — oh sit! Oh Jack I never thought you'd probably ever stop by here to see me and now, oh shit man — oh god man — this is so fucking big and so fucking nice! Oh man — what a dick! Oh Jack — man alive — oh man, I cannot believe this! Oh shit Jack, I cannot believe it yet, that you had all of this great big thick rod of yours, up and inside of my ass the other night! Even standing here now, looking at it, I still can't believe you had all of that up in me! Shit man, I would have never thought my ass could take that much of anything up in there! Oh Jack, when can we get together again man — when can we do that!? I can't believe it, but man — I need it again, I do! Right now my ass is twitching for it! It wants to feel that thing getting pushed up in there again! I wanna feel you spreading my ass open and pushing it up in there! Man, I can't believe that I've only played around once, and all of a sudden, I can't do without it! I need it again man, I do!"

And as I asked, and then realized that he had already made my dick as hard as his was, yeah not as big, but just as hard, and mine was still inside of my work pants, he said, "Well guy, that's one of the reasons I stopped by. To see just when you wanna."

"Oh shit man, shit! Jack, whenever, whenever! Jack I'm sure that getting the time to do it is harder for you than it is for me — you got a wife and kids to worry about, so you tell me!"

"How do you know I got kids to worry about? How do you know that?"

"Oh, I asked Bill the other night. I had to find out just some stuff about you and Bill so that I just knew a little something and I didn't feel like you guys were just plain strangers to me. He told me he's 46! Is that true? Is he really?"

"Yeah, pretty damn good looking and well built for a guy that age, ain't he?"

"Yeah and he's pretty damn well hung too! He fucked the hell out of me after you left! Damn it felt good up in there, and almost as good as having this great big thing stuck up in there! Seriously, I really had not seen his dick until you left — when he got up and off of that mat. Man, both of you guys are fucking hot guys! Fucking hot!"

"Thanks, and I will admit, you ain't no fucking fairy yourself! I'm getting real anxious to see just how you can do sucking on this stick you're playing with right now. You anxious to see how that goes for you? I don't mean now, not now. We need to do that sometime when we can go nice and slow. I don't want you swallowing all of it too fast. I want you to take your time on it!"

"Holy shit man, holy shit! I really don't think there is gonna be any problems of me swallowing that fucking big thing too fast, I sure as hell don't! Hell man. I just hope that when I try it, I just hope I can get my mouth open far enough to just get the tip of it in. That's one fucking big stick man, one hell of a fucking big rod! Seriously Jack, I really didn't know a man could have a cock that big, I didn't!"

"Hey I know it's kinda big man, but it's been stuck in a lot of mouths, and I ain't found one yet that can't take at least most of it! You'll do it, you'll do it!"

Turning my head around some and looking toward the office door, I said, "I'm sorry man but I'm so afraid that Jimmy might come walking back in earlier than I expected. Doing this here is really making me nervous."

"Yeah, I agree." Jack then let loose of my dick, and then completely "undid" his pants and let 'em fall, so that he could push his boner down enough to get his pants back up and around it.

"Uh, Troy, I've got some rather free time tonight — after about nine for a couple of hours or so, you interested? Can you do that?"

"Oh shit yes man, shit yes! I'll get out of here, and get home and get all cleaned up and hell yes man, hell yes! We are gonna do it at my place I assume, right? I mean, we can't go out in the park at that time, so my place, right?"

"Yeah, if that's okay with you. I really didn't know if we were gonna be able to use your place or not, cause I didn't know if you live alone, with a gal or a roommate, of just what!"

"No, I live alone. Not a very big place, but hey man, I plan on being up and pretty damn close to you anyway! We won't need too much space!"

"So this address you gave me the other night is the right address? Right? Apartment number 24?"

"Yeah man, yeah! Shit yes man shit yes! There is no way in hell that I would ever give you the wrong address! Just the idea that you even showed up here today and did what you did, and then set it up that we're gonna get together tonight, hell no man — no way in hell I would have ever given you any bad info!"

"Hey guy — uhhh one other thing before I go. The next day after our little play in the park thing, Bill told me that when he gave you his card and you saw his last name, you told him you know Scotty, right?"

"Yeah, yeah I do. Scotty and I played football together for two years till he transferred over to West Side, and yeah we know each other. Haven't seen him in probably three or four years, but I hear he is still around! Why?"

"Oh, so you don't see him all the time then?"

"No, no! Haven't seen him for quite awhile now, why?"

"Well Bill said something about you asking him if he's seen Scotty's dick lately. You've seen it I guess?"

"Well yeah! When we played together on the same team, we showered together, and even back then, he was hung better than the rest of us, and then one night, like the last time I saw him, he and I did a double date with two gals from over in Citywide, and we all four kinda ended up in a big bed together, and the girls went fucking crazy over his dick! Yeah, I gotta admit that was the only time I ever saw it hard, and yes man, it is a biggie! Hell man, I felt kinda left out once they saw it. Why — why you asking?"

So that night — all of you four in a bed together — did you and he do anything together?"

"No, hell no man — no! I never did anything with any guy until you and I and Bill did it! That was the very first time I ever did anything with a guy!"

Then looking at Jack rather seriously I asked, "Hey wait a minute here man! What are you asking? Did Bill ask you to find out if I and Scotty did something together? Did he ask you that?"

"No Troy, no he didn't ask, but I saw Scotty in a real tight pair of swim trunks a couple of years ago, and ever since then I've wondered about him, and the way his dad is hung — I was wondering if, and kinda figured, he has gotta be hung like his dad — that's all. And yeah, I've always wished he would kinda give me some kinda indication that maybe I could get him off to the side someplace, and make a hit on him. He's hot and yeah, ever since I saw that pair of trunks on him, I've wanted to do something, but just can't!"

"Were you hoping that maybe Scotty and I had done something together? Is that what you were hoping?"

"Yeah, yeah I guess so. Ever since that day when I saw what he was trying to pack in those trunks, I've always kinda wondered about him — not that he ever did anything to make me think he was gay, but hey — you know, once in awhile, a guy's gotta dream. That's all, that's all."

"But what you're saying is — if you got a chance, you'd go for it, right?"

"Yeah hell yes man — hell yes! And after our little session the other night, I'm pretty well convinced that if you ever got a chance at it, you'd go for it too. So — just so we understand each other — if you ever, ever do anything with that guy, you gotta let me know he plays, and you gotta get me together with him! Okay?"

"Yeah, but Jack, I never see him anymore, anywhere!"

"Yeah, I know Troy, I know, but you never know when something can happen! Since you kinda know Bill now, I just thought maybe if you ever happen to see Scotty, and if you can ever kinda maybe make something happen between you two, I just wanna get in on the action, that's all!"

"Yeah, okay, okay — but I really don't know how anything is gonna happen since I never see him anymore! I just never see him."

I stood there and watched Jack finish tucking everything in, and just shook my head at what a beautiful sight he was. I could not believe that he was actually gonna be coming over to my house that night, and was gonna let me play with him and that enormous dick and that beautiful ass of his again!

Reaching down and grabbing ahold of my dick one more time, which then made me do the very same thing back to him, Jack said, "Hey guy, I gotta get going. I gotta go finish my shift and then get myself all ready for some good hot stuff with my new play buddy here, and then get over there and teach him some new stuff! Okay? That okay with you?"

"Oh shit yes man! Shit yes! Hey, pretty soon after nine? That right?"

"Yeah, I should be over there right about nine. You be all ready for me man — I need that ass of yours again — I do!"

Just hearing him say, "I need that ass of yours again, I do!" just about made me collapse right where I was! The rest of my day could not go by fast enough!

I got old man Jamison's Merc. all tuned up, worked on a couple of other smaller projects, and closed things down about seven thirty or a quarter to eight and headed for my place. Everything went pretty well the rest of the day, except for my call to Shirley and lying to her about why I was gonna have to skip our getting together that night, which was not a really good thing, because of the night before. I really did have some major problems keeping a good hardon while we were doing our thing! Being in bed with her, and wishing it was either Jack or Bill that I was in bed with, was a problem. So now, telling her that I was gonna be busy — that was not a good conversation! Right then I was glad I lived in an apartment and my place didn't have a driveway out front where a person could drive by to see it somebody was there or not. Shirley was not a happy child as she hung up!

Five minutes after nine, and my heart beat when I heard the first knock on my front door.

Trying to look hot and sexy for my hot cop man, I opened the door wearing just a kinda tight — and an older pair, of white gym shorts. Some shorts that did really kinda point out my more favorable asset — the one right down in front — in the ole crotch area. Of course when I put 'em on to see if I could still wear 'em, I didn't have a hardon on, and showing, but when that first knock on the door hit, so did my dick!

"Holy shit man, shit! Troy you look good man, you look good man! You look a hell of a lot different than you did this morning at the shop! Man, your shop's business would pick up one hell of a lot if you worked looking like that! That's hot man! Look at that dick sticking out there man, look at that dick!"

Jack came in, I closed the door, and immediately hit the lock on it so that I knew damn well that nobody — nobody, could come walking in unexpectedly!

Except for being completely bare, this was the first time that I had seen Jack in something different than his police uniform, and damn — he was hot! Hot, hot, hot! Fucking damn hot!

He had a white t-shirt on and a pair of Levi's, both of which looked like they had been specially made for that fucking hot tight muscled body of his! And that white shirt, against that mahogany skin, was a complete showpiece! No man, no man anywhere, was hotter than this guy was, and just the idea that within minutes, I was gonna be fucking around with this man and this body was really more than I could imagine.

Ever since he had stopped into the shop earlier that day, my mind had gone totally crazy with thoughts and ideas of what we were gonna be doing together later that night. All day long I just kept having these visions of his face up in my ass, and yeah — my face up in his ass! All day, about all I could think of was my face pushed up and in, and my tongue licking at and around his tight asshole like he had done to mine. I really wanted to feel his hard ass cheeks pushing up against my face, and I wanted to feel my tongue pushing out and reaching for his hole. I wanted to feel my tongue sticking up in that tight hole as far as I could get it to go.

I reached over, slid my hands up and under his tight white t-shirt, pinched both his left nipple and his right nipple, smiled at him and said, "Come on big man, come on! I want everything now, right now — everything that I didn't get the other night! I need you, and I need all of you now — right now! You are gonna do me man, you are gonna do me, and I know damn well I'm gonna be begging for more before you are done! One session with you out in the park, and you have turned me into the hungriest gay whore guy around! I need you man! I need you up and in me and eating me out just as much as you can. I wanna feel you biting on my butt, and my ass rim and I want you to bite my tits tonight too man — yeah, I do! Come on, let's go in here, come on!"

Chapter Four

And to Slap My Face Hard With It!

I was standing there just huffing and puffing like crazy, just wanting to get my man into the bedroom and get him in bed with me, or maybe — me in bed with him! Whichever, whatever, I sure as hell did not care — just in bed together!

I'd had some pretty sexy times with some of my gals in the past, and there were some times when I was damn sure that I was having the epitome of sex that any person could have, but I found out, by playing with my big black cop, I hadn't even started living life in the sex lane yet!

It only took me a second to strip off the tiny little shorts that I had on, and I flopped down on my back on the bed as I watched Jack start to pull up on the bottom of his t-shirt and start pulling it up and over his head. Just the first slight movement of that shirt coming up and showing that tight washboard stomach and that beautiful belly button, made my dick get even harder and harder as that shirt went up higher and higher, and Jack started stretching up his arms and starting to show me in the most magnificent way, the undersides of his arms and all of the hard solid muscles that he had wrapped up in that beautiful mahogany skin!

With his hands stretched up high and every bit of that beautiful solid upper body showing — as if he was on a muscleman posing platform, I thought I was gonna shoot some cum shots without even touching my dick! I just laid there and took one big deep breath, after another, trying to realize that, that man, that one hell of a hunk of a man, was actually getting ready to come and get in bed with me! In bed — totally nude — with a major hardon sticking out in front, showing everything, and then letting me play with it, and then he playing with me! I truly did not think that I was even close to the quality of a man that could be getting this hunk of a man, to even pay any attention to me, let alone getting played with by him. I wanted his hands on me! I did, right away! Just the thought that he was gonna be getting in bed with me was so fucking exciting, that I wanted him to just jump in bed with me and start feeling me all over, and letting me feel all of him. I wanted to feel parts of him that I'd never felt before. Yeah, I wanted to feel his insides! I wanted to put my fingers up in his ass!

I truly thought for a second or two that I was going into some kind of a panic attach or something, just laying there and looking at the man, the most gorgeous man I had ever seen! His tinny solid tight waist, the beautiful belly button, the ripples in his gut, the enormous V shape of his lats, the muscles in his arms and yes, even his beautiful face and head as he pulled the t-shirt up and off!

As I laid there and watched that shirt come up and off of Jack's face and his head, I truly could not comprehend that I was actually going to be having that face and that head pushed up into my butt and it was gonna be my ass that was gonna be feeling his tongue licking me and my hole! No way in hell could I imagine that, that man, that body, that structure, those muscles and that face were actually gonna be licking on my asshole, when that whole image of him, could actually be the cover picture of some hot hunk male magazine! A man that truly could be on the cover of an international weightlifter magazine for millions and millions of people to look at, was actually gonna be the man that puts his face up and in my ass — is going to be licking my ass — is going to be sticking his tongue up and in my asshole, and yes — thank God — I was gonna get to do the same thing to him!

Jack slid his arms and his hands out of his t-shirt and threw it to the side, onto a chair. He dropped his arms down, and I wilted! My eyes could not see everything fast enough! My heart was pounding, and my blood pressure had to be sky high! My whole body was about to go into total shock! I remembered the very first time I had sex with a girl, and I thought I was excited and about to loose control then, but my excitement then, was nothing to what I was going through now! I was becoming a complete basket case just laying there watching him get undressed!

Each second, each movement, gave me that much more totally, out-of-control excitement! I wanted him to be a steamroller and roll all over me! Truly I wanted him just all over me, suffocating me and making me part of him, or him part of me! I wanted to feel him, all of him, every inch of him, and let him feel me! He was so fucking hot, so damn hot I could not believe I was actually watching him, and even more so, that he was in my bedroom, and was getting ready to get in bed with me, and fuck me — let me fuck him — eat me out — let me eat him out — chew on my tits — let me chew on his tits — suck me off and the really, really, big, big point — I was gonna get to suck on that dick of his, and on that bag of balls of his, or whatever part of that dick or that bag of balls, that it I could get into my mouth! His dick was so big I knew it was gonna be like sucking on the thick end of a baseball bat, and his nuts were so big, I knew they were gonna be like trying to chew on two big Idaho potatoes, at the same time!

He didn't even have his Levi's off yet, and me just the knowing what I had been fucked with, three days earlier, made me go fucking crazy! I hadn't even seen it yet that night — the dick — nor the balls, yet I was turning wild hog crazy wanting to feel it in me, on me, and any other way that he wanted to use it on me. I had never been slapped in the face with a guy's dick before, but all of a sudden, I wanted slapped with his dick, and I wanted it slapped hard! I wanted that enormous rod of his to come snap out of those Levi's and just slap the hell out of my face! The whole idea of him standing there, his eleven inches, or whatever enormous length it gets to, when it's hot, sticking out toward me, him taking ahold of it and slamming it back and forth across my face, hitting my face with it, was making me go crazy. I had never, ever, heard of a man getting slapped in the face with some other guy's dick, but right then, the whole idea of getting slapped by that dick was almost way too much to handle. I had never thought about getting slapped on my face, by a man's dick, but right then, it was becoming the most important thing in my life! I really wanted to feel it hitting the sides of my face — back and forth — back and forth! I really didn't know if gay guys did that to each other or not, but I didn't care! I wanted it, and I knew I wanted it bad! I knew I wanted to be able to know the next morning, when I got up, that I had been face whipped by Jack and his big dick! The whole idea of going into the bathroom in the morning, to look at my face to see if it had any bruised or black and blue marks on it from his dick hitting it, made me real turned on! I knew that before he left my place that night, I would beg him, and beg him hard, to slap my face with it, and to slap my face hard with it!

Jack unbuttoned the top button on his Levi's and just in anticipation of knowing that I was gonna be seeing it again, in just a second, I took one hell of a big breath! I'd seen it before, and I'd felt it up in my ass before, and right then I was thanking God that it was all gonna be happening again! I had been so fucking afraid that, that last Tuesday night, was gonna be a one time thing, and until Jack showed up at my shop earlier that day, I was really in doubt that I would ever get to see it and feel it again! And, right then — I was just about to see it and feel it again! Oh my day was glorious! It was way more than any man could ask for! Well, yeah, that enormous big rod of Jack's was more than any man could ask for too, and thank goodness — I was gonna be the guy getting to play with it, and — get poked in the ass with it! I was in heaven, true heaven!

Jack unbuttoned the top button, then leaned down to pull off his gym shoes and socks, and of course I was given the most beautiful view of the best-built ass on this side of the continent! Levi's or not, there is no way in hell that, that ass, and all of the muscles in that ass, could not be classified as the hottest ass anyway, on anybody, regardless of age or size! It was perfect, fucking perfect, and yeah — I especially like the "fucking" part of it! I knew I was gonna get to fuck that ass, and I was out of my mind just thinking about it! I'd fucked Bill that night in the park, and now I was gonna get to fuck the other hot muscled ass that I had watched, from my little cover spot in the cemetery! That night, until I finally stripped everything off and presented myself all bare and naked, and with a hardon showing, I never thought that there would ever be a time and a place where I'd even be seeing it again, let alone sticking my dick up in it! That night, out in the park, just watching this ass going up and down and tightening up and loosening up while he was fucking Bill's ass was part of the whole reason I finally stripped everything off and came out of hiding. That ass — man — that ass! I'd never seen anything that ever got me turned on as much as watching that hot tight ass pumping up and down on Bill's butt!

After I appeared, I got to fuck Bill's ass, but while they were fucking, that was the first and only time that I had ever seen two men making out with each other, let alone one of them sticking his cock up in the other guy's ass, and pounding the hell out of it! While I was still hiding, that just made me and my head swim in circles realizing what in the hell I was watching! Never before that night, only three days ago, had I ever seen something like that, and now, in my own bedroom, I was gonna get to pound that tight muscled ass just like he pounded Bill's and that was way, beyond belief! I had fucked Bill's ass, and now I was gonna get it from the other big guy and I was gonna get to fuck him too!

Jack got his shoes and socks off, stood up, looked at me and grinned! Once again, I took a big deep breath and then I grinned back at him. It might have been a grin, but inside of me I was yelling, "Hurry up man, hurry up!"

Hell, it couldn't have been more than probably one minute since we had gotten into the bedroom and he started taking stuff off and showing me the hottest fucking skin show that had been done in years, but to me, it had felt like an hour. My body, my hands, my mouth, my dick, everything of me, all of me, wanted that man in bed beside me and touching me!

In my mind, all too slowly, but in reality, at normal moving speed, Jack slid his fingers in the top of his Levi's and all too slowly started to move 'em down. I had already known from the minute that I opened the front door that he was not wearing any briefs, and the sight of that dick, hanging down about eight inches, still soft, inside of his left pants leg had made me a complete whore for dick — his dick, and if it had been out on the street, yes, I would have offered to pay HIM, to let me get at it! How in the hell a man can even walk down an apartment sidewalk showing that much dick pushing out on the side of, and through the denim pants leg of a pair of Levi's, and get away with it, I will never know! With the thickness of that rod, he might as well have just walked in naked and letting it hang out and swing! I know damn well, that if he had passed anybody on his way from the parking lot, that person was now "in heat!" Man or woman, regardless of who, anyone that saw that much stick hanging down inside of a pair of Levi's — they had to be walking away horny as hell!

As he pulled his Levi's down, way too slow for my mind, I started to once again see that very precious part of a man's body that the public can only wish they could see, and yet they talk about as if they saw it all of the time! His skin, his beautiful tight mahogany skin!

Jack pulled his Levi's down slightly, then reached in and pulled his now, hard, firm, stiff, fat, baseball bat of a dick up and out of the top of his pants! I took another big life saving breath. It was hard! It wasn't the previous soft eight inches any more! It was at least eleven inches long and it had to be fatter around than a coke can or a beer can! It was fucking gorgeous — fucking gorgeous! And that from a guy that three days earlier, would have probably slugged you if you had suggested that I'd ever do anything with a man!

I swear! His dick was bigger then, than it had been earlier in the day, when he had it out and we were both playing with it in the shop. Yeah, I had jerked on it, and stroked it, and rubbed it — but he had done the same thing too, just to make me as hot as hell for it. Little did he know that just my remembering it from last Tuesday night, out in the park, made me get a fucking ragging hardon for it! Whenever I thought about that thing, and especially about it going up in my ass, I actually had to kind of shake my head and bring myself back to reality! Nothing, in my entire life, had made as much of an effect on me and my way of living, as that big dick, hanging down on cop Jack, had done! Ever since that Tuesday night, well actually early Wednesday morning, after our session in the park, I had not been able to keep my mind on anything else, I just kept seeing Jack's dick in my mind!

He finally pulled his Levi's down past the Southwestern Electric Telephone pole that was standing out and up, and pointing directly toward me!

All my mind could do right then was, silently, keep yelling, "Hurry up man, hurry up!"

To me it felt like it had taken him all night, which was really probably less than a minute and a half total, but he was finally leaning over me, putting both hands up beside my head, his left knee on the bed beside me, and then the right knee on the bed also. He, — THE man, THE hunk, THE god, THE dream of any person that loves sex, was up above me, now over me and leaning down — kissing me!

Jack was kissing me as if he did this to me all of the time. He was kissing me all over my head, all over my face, all over my neck, and he was now leaning down and kissing my left tit!

"Oh Jack bite it man, please bite it! Jack I saw you biting on Bill's tit the other night, please bite me man, please!"

Oh my gawd man, it did not take two requests to ask him to bite me! Wow! Man alive, I was finally getting my tit bit like I had kinda dreamed about out in the cemetery when I saw Jack and Bill biting on each other. I remembered that when I watched them biting on each other, I had thought then, "—now I gotta admit that since I like to do some of the rougher stuff in life — just to know I can do it and then tell people I did it, maybe I needed to try getting my tits bitten on and my nuts clamped down on real hard! Yeah, right! Do it! Who in the hell am I gonna tell, that I got my tits and my nuts chewed on by some strong mouthed man?"

Who in the hell cares, who in the hell I could tell that I had been bitten on and chewed on like that? Who in the fucking hell cares! I was getting it, well at least right then getting my tits chewed on, and I did not give a damn if anybody knew it or not! I knew it — Jack knew it, and I'm sure we'd tell Bill sometime too, cause I knew I'd want him biting on me too, and other than us three, who in the hell cares! I just know that right then I was proving to my man, my sexier than shit cop man, that I could take it, and I could beg for more! I was just starting to prove to my man, that I could play with the big boys! And in my mind, I had to prove that! I had to prove that to Jack — and to me, too!

"Oh Jack, yeah man, yeah! Yeah Jack, bite 'em man, bite 'em. I wanna know I can take it like Bill does! Bite me man, bite me! Bite my tit man — bite my tit! Bite 'em, bite 'em!! Oh god man — yeah keep it up — oh keep it up! Yeah man, yeah man!"

I don't know why in the hell I ever thought I needed to tell Jack to bite me, he was biting the hell out of me! He was biting my tit and sucking damn near half of my pec up into his mouth! I felt his biting going all the way through my body! It even made my balls shake and move! I loved it, I did! It went through my whole body! What a fucking feeling. Something I had never felt before, never!

"Oh Jack — oh man — I love that man — I love that! Bite it man, bite it! Suck that tit man — suck that tit! Oh do it man, do it!"

I finally had my big cop up and on top of me, and he was finding out that I wanted to do some of the big boy stuff, and as he bit and chewed, he also started some finger fucking up in my ass.

I saw him reach over to the bed table, dip the fingers of his right hand in the bowl of grease, that I had smartly thought to put out before he arrived, and when I saw that grease on his fingers, I knew damn well that my ass was just about to get some action. I had the grease there cause I knew, sure as hell, I did not want him trying to put that dick of his up in my ass without a lot of grease on it — and up in my ass!

Oh shit man, just the sight of that grease on his fingers turned me on like a ragging lion. I wanted it, and I need it. Something — anything — up in my ass!

Now with Jack resting down on top of me a little more, not quite up so high, I could feel him laying across my gut and my chest as he chewed and bit on my tits, and much to my complete pleasure, I also felt, not one finger enter, but two fingers going in my ass, right off of the bat! I was now impaled with two of the hottest fucking fingers in the state! Hell man — any and every part of that man, to me, is gonna be the hottest part in the state. He slid the fingers up in nice and smoothly, and then immediately he let me know they were up and in there by letting them roam around and feel all of the insides of my ass! Oh shit man, I was in haven. My tits, both of 'em were getting bitten and chewed on, and sucked on, and now my ass was, for the very first time in my life, knowing what it felt like to have a man's fingers up in there and roaming around! On last Tuesday night, he had stuck a finger up on there, but that was while I was fucking Bill, and I really, really did not know exactly what was going on back there, well that is until I realized that Jack had stuck his whole fucking dick up inside of me! That freaked me out until I found out that I had already taken all of it, and there sure wasn't any more for him to push up in me. I remember I figured, "I got the whole damn thing up inside of me, enjoy it man, enjoy it!"

Jack reached over, grabbed a tissue off of the night stand, wiped his fingers off some, wiped my ass some, then took ahold of both of my legs and threw them up in the air, and let my asshole get exposed as if it was gonna get its picture taken.

He held my legs up, and kinda back over the top off my head, and immediately I felt his tongue going up and into my asshole! Oh man! Oh man! What can a guy say when that happens? I threw my head up, and back, and just let out a steady stream of, "Oh yeah, oh yeah, oh yeah, oh yeah!" Oh man, I was in haven! My ass felt like it was up in the sky, looking and acting like one big puffy cloud! I could not believe how this man could push his face so fucking far up into my ass, and be able to get his tongue out far enough to actually stick, probably two inches of it, up and into my ass! Oh man, what a great feeling, what a feeling!!

I could feel Jack's face pushing up against the cheeks of my ass! I closed my eyes and I tried to imagine what that looked like. My ass, my bare ass and his face pushed up in there so tightly that his entire face would be hidden. Never in my entire life, had I ever thought that I'd be into getting sucked in the ass by some guy, and shit-as-hell-man, never by some hot built muscled black patrolman, that could, if he had reason to, could put handcuffs on me, and throw me in jail for some reason or another!

A cop, a hot fucking cop was sucking out my ass! Oh man, the thoughts that were going through my mind! Yeah, I know he had done that out in the park too, in the middle of the night, in the dark, but this time, he had actually come over to my apartment to do it! He wanted to do it! Oh shit man, how in the hell can I ever realize what was happening to me! Me, I was the big man around town, the one fucking every little lady that asked, and now I am the one that is getting it, and wanting more of it, and it's not with some freaking gal — it's with one of the world's hottest cops — and he's at my place doing it! He's in my apartment and in my bed, and now in my ass!

His face is in my ass and his tongue is in my hole, and there is no way in hell that I could ask for anything better — except for maybe having Bill there too, and having both of these hot studly, big built, and big hung cops, doing stuff to me all at the same time again! I knew I was really liking the idea that I was really being their toy to play with, and to let them do anything they wanted to do with me. Use me! I had always been the big man and people did what I wanted, and now I was the one being used, and I loved it! With these two hot hunky men, how in the hell could a man ever say no? He had to love it! I sure as fucking hell knew I loved it!

Oh I knew right then that I had to get that three-man play, set up. I really needed to have both of those guys doing some really wild, sexy stuff with me, and with my body, and all at the same time again. Before last Tuesday night in the park, I had never had my body played with like this, and man, I never thought that any man could feel this good by having some other guy sucking and biting on him and doing everything else that can be done to a body! Even on the football field, with guys piling up on top of me, I never felt this kind of excitement — wanting my body played with — sucked on — bitten on — pulled on, and stuffed full, back in my ass area, like all of a sudden I was wanting — in every way possible! I was totally horny for my man to use me

63

and abuse me and my body, anyway he wanted! I really wanted him to have fun, some real serious fun, with me and my body and all of its parts! Inside I just kept yelling, "Take me — use me and abuse me! Be a rough cop to me man, be a real rough cop on me man!"

I knew that before this session was over, I was gonna be begging Jack to take ahold of that big dick of his and slap me across the face with it, and I will probably be yelling, "Harder man, — harder man," and then, I will finally get to do some sucking on that great big black dick! Or at least suck as much of it as I can get in my mouth! Hell man, he's got me so fucking hot and horny for me getting everything done to me, I'm sure that once I get a chance to get the tip of that rod in my mouth, I'm gonna probably choke myself half to death taking all of it, all of the way down in my throat! Man I want that thing down in me now, and I want him to push hard getting it in me! I want him to grab the back of my head, hang onto my head and force it in me, down in my throat! I can take it up in the ass, and I wanna take all of it down in my throat — and I wanna do it the very first time he sticks it in there! I want my virgin mouth to take the whole fucking thing!

Then maybe, when I can get all three of us together again, I can suck on one of 'em — and get him all the way down in my throat while the other one fucks my ass, and goes up in my ass just as far as he can go, and gives me all of his dick, back in that end of me too! Oh shit, just the idea of seeing if I can get something set up so that I can get fucked in both ends at once and then maybe get both of 'em to slap my face with both of their big dicks at the same time! Oh shit man — oh shit!! Oh man, the ideas that are running through my head! And only three days ago — I would have never even thought about some guy doing that to some other guy, let alone — that guy being me! Oh man I have found my real self, and no wonder I have always gotten so rough with all of my girl playmates! I was finally realizing I liked sex rough, and I liked it rough on me! I was finally finding sex, some good rough sex, sex that really uses me and my body! Sex that somebody else controls and makes me do their thing, getting their rocks off for their joy!

"Oh Jack — Jack that feels so fucking good back there man — so fucking good! Suck on my hole man, suck on my hole! Bite it man — bite it! Chew my hole man — chew on my hole!! Oh Jack get my hole ready for your dick man — get my hole ready! Jack, I want your fucking big dick up in me man — I want you to fuck my asshole man, I do! I want you to pound my ass man — I do! Rough! I want you to pound me rough! I want you to pound my ass rough man, real rough! I want you to push that fucking big dick of yours up in my ass man — I wanna feel it man, I do! I wanna feel you pulling my ass open so you can push it up in there man, I do! Bite me man, bite me! Make my hole feel you man — bite my hole! Oh Jack — oh Jack! Oh Jack I need you to fuck me man! I need you to fuck me! I gotta get fucked by you man, I gotta get fucked! Jack, Jack! My ass is so fucking hungry for your dick right now man, you gotta fuck me or I gotta find something big to put up in my ass! I gotta get fucked man, I gotta! I gotta feel you pushing up in man, I do! I gotta feel you and that great big dick of yours up in me! Fuck me man, fuck me!"

Chapter Five

Flip Over Man!

I was laying there on my back — Jack had his face pushed up against my ass so tight, I couldn't even believe that I was almost yelling at him to fuck me! How in the hell can any man try to tell some hot, built, hunk like Jack to stop biting and chewing on his ass, and tell him to fuck him instead? How in the hell, I don't know, but I did!

My ass was so fucking hungry from all of Jack's chewing on it and eating on it that I was turning inside out with just the desires of feeling that enormous big thick stick of meat of his, going back up in my ass like it did out in the park, last Tuesday night.

"Hey Troy my guy, flip over! Flip over and lay on your gut! I'm gonna give you what you want, and I want you laying there nice and straight so that my rod can go up in you just as smooth as possible. I gotta get everything inside of you all good and straight, so I can drive my dick right in there and let you have it all! Flip over man! I'm gonna fuck your ass! Flip over!"

I did! I guess I must have, cause all I know is, I was on my gut when he did me! And when I say did me, I mean fucked me, and fucked me! My mind was so fucking far out in space that all I know is that he must have told me to flip and I did! My ass was yelling for it! I remember how fucking great it felt that night out in the park, and man I wanted it again, but for some fucking funny reason, I wanted even more than I knew Jack had to give me. I guess I wanted an elephant going up in me, I guess I did! Just one time of getting fucked, and man, it changed my ass into one dick hungry whore hole! I wanted fucked and I wanted it rough! I could not believe that after only getting fucked in the ass once, my ass was so fucking hungry for something really big going back up in it!

"Lay still guy, lay still! I'm gonna slip some nice smooth grease up in that ass of yours so that I can just slide my dick up in you, nice and smooth! Lay there and get ready man, I'm gonna stick my dick back up in there like I did the other night! Remember the other night man — remember the other night? You had my dick all the way up in you — all the way up in there! For a virgin ass that night, you sure did take it, and you took all of it! You wanting it again — I guess! You wanting it up in there again? You and your ass ready man — you ready?"

"Oh fuck yes man, fuck yes! Oh Jack I need that dick of yours up in me man, I need it! I took it the other night and I want it again! Oh Jack, fuck me man — fuck me! Please put it up in me man, please put it up in me! I wanna feel it going up in me, I gotta feel your dick up in me again man — I do! I want it up in me, I want it up in me! Fuck me man — please fuck me!"

"I am Troy guy — I am. Feel the tip of it up against your hole? You just lay there nice and quiet for a minute and you'll be getting it — believe me man — I wanna stick it up in you just as bad as you want it! I wanna feel your tight ass grabbing onto it man, I do! Lay still there, lay still. Yeah, yeah, I just felt the tip of it go in you — I did. I just popped the tip of my cock in you — now just lay still man — lay there and take my dick! I want your ass!!"

"Oh Jack — oh Jack! Yeah man, yeah you just went in! I felt it, I felt it go in — yeah I did! Oh my God I did — I did! You're in me man, I know it, I feel it! Oh Jack I am so fucking anxious for you to drill me man, I want it so bad! Jack please push it in me man — OH SHIT — OOOH SHIT — oh man — oh shit, oh, oh, oh shit man, oh shit! Oh shit, oh God man — oh God, — oh shit Jack you just pushed it in all the way in me, didn't you? I just took the whole fucking thing didn't I? I took all of it — didn't I!? You pushed all of it up and in me didn't you? You gave it all to me didn't you Jack? You pushed all of it in me — all at once didn't you!? Oh God man, oh God! Oh Jack — oh shit! Oh man, I can't believe you just gave me the whole fucking thing! You fucked me all the way, didn't you? Oh Jack, my God man — oh shit! Ohhhhhhh shit man, ohhhhh shit! Oh Jack I've got all of your big fucking dick up in me right now, don't I, Jack? I've got all of it up in me now don't I, Jack? I can't believe I took all of it that fast! I've got all of it up in me, don't I? Ohhhh shit man — ohhhh shit! Oh God man, I've got all of your big fucking dick up inside of me don't I? Oh man, you went in me so fast! So fucking fast! I've got your whole dick, don't I? Don't I? I took the whole thing didn't I? The whole thing?"

"Yes you did man, yes you did! You okay? You okay? Did that hurt? Troy, did that hurt?"

"No, no! No it didn't really hurt too much, it didn't really hurt too much! But oh man, I can't believe you put that much dick up in me so fast! Oh God, I took all of it so fucking fast! Oh Jack I can't believe you put that whole fucking dick up in me that fast! I took all of it that fast? Jack did I really take all of it that fast!? Have you got all of it up in me? Have I got all of you up in me?"

"Yeah you got it man, you got it! You took all of it man, you took all of it! I got the head of it all lined up at your hole and you kept telling me that you wanted it — you wanted it, you kept begging me to fuck you — so I figured that if your ass was that fucking hungry for it, then I figured I'd let you have it! You okay? You okay Troy?"

As I laid there grabbing onto both sides of the mattress and slamming my head up and down on the pillow, I tried to tell Jack that I was okay, but at the same time I was pushing my ass back, just plain begging for more and more dick. I knew he had the whole fucking thing up in my ass, but I still wanted more! Within three short days, my ass had turned so fucking dick hungry that I wasn't sure there was anything big enough, anywhere, that was ever gonna satisfy my ass and its hunger for big dick. When I thought earlier, just a few seconds earlier that I was wondering if I wanted an elephant up in there — now I was really wondering. Jack's dick was obviously the biggest dick that I was ever gonna get poked up in there, and for some sick reason, I wanted more up in me, in farther, and pushing out the sides of my ass even more! My ass was so fucking hungry for some big wild action, I started wondering just what in the hell could satisfy me.

"Oh Jack, pound it man, pound it! Pound my ass man, pound my ass! Make my ass hurt man, make it hurt! Pound it fucking hard man, — drill me — pound on it! Oh Jack fuck me rougher than any guy you've ever fucked before man, do it, — do it — drill me! Make me part of you man, make me part of you!"

I laid there and heard myself begging my big cop, the man with the eleven or twelve inch big dick, to drill my ass, and I started wondering if I was trying to get into something more than I could handle! He started slamming on my butt like it was some kind of a rock smasher tearing down the side of a mountain. Oh shit man, it felt good! My whole body was bouncing up and down — up and down! I was really having some trouble trying to catch my breath, but there was no way in hell that I was gonna tell my man of rock hard steel — up there on my back — and in my butt, to stop! I was getting what I had been yelling for, and I was liking it! I was loving it! I was kinda wishing there were really two guys up there doing that to me, if it could have made the actions inside of me that much better! I actually could feel some of my guts moving back and forth every time big Jack's cock came slamming back into my ass! I don't know, cause I couldn't see back there, but I think Jack must have been pulling all the way up, almost taking the tip of his dick out of my ass, then slamming back down into me as fast and as hard as he could! That was taking about eleven or twelve inches of his big thick stiff dick almost all the way out, and then all of a sudden, slamming the whole damn thing back down in me! Damn it felt good! I was getting fucked, and I was getting fucked the way I wanted it! Rough, fucking rough! I wanted to be one of the "big boys," and I think this was making me one of the "big boys." Fact is, I really doubted that most of the "big boys," so to say, could take it or even want to take it, as rough as I was getting from my big patrolman right then!

"Oh shit man, oh shit! Hey Troy ole man, hang on man, hang on! I'm just about ready to load you full of some hot cop cum man — hang on man, hang on — I'm about to load you up! It's building up in there man, it's building up, it's gonna shoot man, I'm gonna shooooooot! Here it commmes man — here it commmesssss!! Ohh man, ohhhh man!!!"

And with that statement, all of a sudden Jack pushed in on my butt, he threw all of his body right down on top of me, I could feel his legs quiver and I could feel his dick go total rock solid as it shot out some of the hottest cum, that I think any man could shoot. I actually wondered it maybe it burned the inside of his dick before it shot out! It didn't burn my insides, but let me tell you, it felt good — damn good! It gave me feelings like I had never felt before, and I thought everything that last Tuesday night, when he loaded my ass out in the park, felt good! Man it felt like maybe he had been eating some hot sauce just before he started pumping my ass! Damn what a feeling, what a beautiful feeling!

Jack totally collapsed on top of me, and I let my ass squeeze his dick just as tight as I could squeeze! I heard him kind of whisper in my ear something like, "Yeah man, yeah! Squeeze it man, squeeze it. I like that man, I like that. Oh, no pussy can do that man — no pussy can do that!"

Jack was breathing so heavily on my head and my neck that it just turned me on that much more! I absolutely could not believe that within the last there days, I had gone so far away from the female sex stuff over, to where I knew, I'd never be happy with sex unless it was with some big strong and damn well hung guy! All of a sudden I wondered if I was kinda turning into some kind of a funny female myself, knowing that I had to get fucked and I had to have a man laying on top of me, just trying to re-coop after loading my ass with some of the country's greatest man cream! Damn I loved it! My ass was so fucking full of cum and that enormous big black dick, that I just wanted to lay there for days and days! I had never — never in my entire life, enjoyed the feeling of another person being up against me and feeling me and all of my body, all bare, like I was feeling right then!

Jack was laying on top of me and chewing on my earlobe when all of a sudden, he almost yelled, "Oh man, oh man I'm sorry! Oh Troy, I'm sorry guy, I didn't know I was doing that, I didn't! I'm sorry!"

I tried to turn around to him as much as I could and I almost yelled myself when I asked, "Sorry for WHAT? What in the hell you sorry about? Jack I've never in my entire life ever had somebody do that to me, and for me, and make me feel like I do right now! You can chew on that ear any damn time you want to man, any damn time you want! I'm serious man, of all the playmates I've had ever since I took my first piece of pussy, not one time did any of those girls make me feel like you've made me feel right now! I finally feel like I'm in bed with someone that really can love me and not just have sex with me! You can chew on my ear or any other part of me any damn time you wanna. I'll never tell you to stop, I won't!"

And with that, Jack pulled up good and tight to my left ear and after taking the entire ear into his mouth, he sucked the air out of it and bit my entire ear! Damn man! Wow! What a great feeling! I, of course, did not know he was going to do that, but after it happened, there was no way in hell that I was gonna ask him to never do that again! I swear, every minute with this man gave me another new unbelievable sensation! I had never, ever, in my entire life, lived the highs that I was getting by being in bed with this "giant" of a man. I know, he was no giant, but man, if he'd had his dick up in your ass, then maybe you'd know why I called him that!

After we laid there for probably six or seven minutes, and Jack had rolled over and off of my back, he finally asked, "Hey guy, wanna go take a nice cool shower together? I wanna clean this grease off of my rod, cause when we get back in bed, I wanna see just how much of this dick you can take down in your throat, and see if you can take it down your throat as fast as you do up in your ass! Wanna shower together and then maybe help soap me and my ole butt up some?"

Jack handed me the bar of soap, and actually told me to soap him up all over! And I did!

"Hey Troy, take this soap and soap me all up and don't forget my ass. Get it good and soapy and rub it in! Yeah man, yeah, that's what I need."

He allowed me to feel him all over, in every spot and in every way I could. He stood under the spray of water and watched it slide down over his magnificent body, over each and every tight muscle, and watched my hands follow. I stood there in the shower and actually worshiped the body that I was so slowly and so lovingly lathering up and getting all slick and slippery! I grabbed his dick and I soaped it up and then rinsed it off, and then soaped it up all over again. I had to use both hands when I got soap on it, — one hand up by the head of it and the other hand back by the base. It was so fucking long that I could move both hands back and forth on it, like jerking it off, without my hands touching! I stepped up closer and let my bare body slide up and down the front of him, and his manly, strong, big body, and I just let our bodies really feel and touch each other — and at the same time — I let my mind go off into some crazy space, not really being able to realize that my body was actually making skin to skin love, to his magnificent body.

I lifted Jack's right arm up and slid the bar of soap down the full length of his arm, down to his beautiful arm pit, and as I lathered that arm pit up, I then slid my face right up into his pit and moved some of the soap lather around, on the under side of his bicep, and down the side of his rib cage, with my face.

Jack then raised up his left arm, placed it on the upper part of the shower wall and by smiling at me, asked me to do the same thing to his left side as I had done to the right!

I slid the bar of soap out from under his over-muscled right arm and its manly, manly armpit, and slid it across his chest to approach his left arm and the equally exciting left armpit. Once again I put my face right up in that armpit, and moved some of the soap around with my face. And, once again, I worshiped another part of his body and all of the tight stretched mahogany skin that covered his arms, his chest, his rib cage and his lats! I worshiped each and every square inch of that skin and all of the muscles packed inside! Jack stood there and let me reach and rub any and all parts of him that I wanted. He knew he was giving a new gay guy, some real experiences that he was going to remember for the rest of his life! He knew I was actually worshiping the male body for my first time, and he was letting me do it as completely as I could! He was letting me use his body for my total and personal enjoyment!

"Hey, Troy, do my ass. Soap up my ass and make it good and clean, way up in there man, do my ass! Slide that soap and your hands up in that ass crack man, soap me up! You can move that soap around with you face, like you did in my arm pits, if you want!"

He turned around so that his ass end was pointed at me, he leaned up against the shower wall and actually gave me his ass to do with as I pleased! And I did! Man alive did I! This was really the first time that I gotten any chance of getting to his ass and really feeling it like I'd wanted to ever since that last Tuesday night! Muscles, muscles, muscles! Oh man, what an ass! Totally unbelievable to me that a man could have a butt as solid, as round, as filled out and as firm as that ass is of his! There should really be some kind of a law, that an ass like that one cannot be covered up with pants or anything else! We think Mt. Rushmore is outstanding — well more people need to be able to see this sculpture! His ass is one hell of a lot better than most of the art pieces in ancient museums that people pay big money to get in and see. And this piece of art was not behind some fuzzy rope or behind some plate of glass, it was there, three inches from right in front of my face and my mouth, and I was breathing on it! And yes, I moved some of the soap around on it and into the crack of it with my face!

When he handed me the soap and asked me to wash his ass, man my heart just started beating like crazy! I slid that bar of soap up in there and really lathered him and that hot tight muscled ass up good! That was the first time that I had, had a chance to feel his asshole, and to be honest, that was the very first time that I had ever stuck my finger up in any man's ass, and yes — it fucking turned me on!! When he asked me to do his ass, I just knew without even thinking about it, I was gonna go wild! I stooped down right behind his ass and just as soon as I rinsed some of the soap off of it, I grabbed onto both ass cheeks, pulled them apart and pushed my face right up in there, and real close to his asshole. I licked as far in, toward his hole, as I could, but I couldn't reach it with my tongue! I knew I was gonna need to have him either lay down on the bed so I could really force my face up in there, or have him on the bed and on his knees so I could move in on that hole by pulling his cheeks apart and really pressing my face up in there.

But, there, even in the shower, I was feeling my heart beating and pounding stronger that it ever had beat before, in the park or at any other time and place! My face and his ass! I couldn't get over it, that I was putting my face up in another man's ass!

I pushed my face up in that crack just as far as I could push! I stuck my tongue out and I licked the inside of both of his ass cheeks! I loved it! I did! The mere idea that I actually had my face slammed up in the ass end of another man — simply made me shake with bewilderment. Never in my wildest dreams, and even only a few days earlier, would I have ever thought, or had the slightest idea, that I would ever put my face up in some guy's ass. And now, I was doing it and I was having more sexual excitement about doing that than any other action I had ever done. Just the whole idea, that I was doing something so outrageous, was turning me on completely! I was licking, smelling and kissing his ass, and all at the same time that I was wondered just how in the world could I have changed my ways of thinking so far, and so fast! Right then though, I didn't care! All I knew was that if I could have stuck my head up inside of that ass, I would have. I sure was trying, the way I was pushing my face up in there, and the way I was reaching out with my tongue! I wanted to tongue fuck that hot ass so fucking bad! I did!

Jack backed up slightly, and all of a sudden I realized that I was now pinned with my back up against the shower wall, and Jack's ass was pushing on my face. Oh man, alive! What a fucking feeling — what a fucking feeling! I was trapped between the wall and his ass! I could hardly breathe, but I really didn't care. I was getting some really big powerful help in getting my face pushed up in there, and I was loving it! To somebody else — most people, that might sound kinda sick, but I was loving it! My face — in his ass! Wow man, wow! I loved it! I was so glad he was pushing back on my face that way! He had a hand on each butt cheek, and he was pulling them apart, so that he could push his ass right up on my face!

After standing there and pushing back on my face and feeling my tongue finally reach in far enough to reach his asshole, Jack moved forward, and said. "Hey man, let's rinse off, get dried off some and get back in that bed. You've finally gotten to my ass, I felt your tongue go up in there a little, and now I wanna see just how much of my dick I can get down that throat of yours. You ready to do some cock sucking man? Never had a dick in your mouth, right?"

"No, no Jack, no! No man, like I told you, the only man-to-man playing around I've ever done was with you and Bill the other night, that's all. But Jack, I want it, and I want as much of it as I can get! Come on, let's get in bed, I wanna see what I can do. I've gotta know I took your dick in my mouth tonight! I gotta do that!"

And with that statement, we toweled off, I wiped his ass and his dick, and he did the same for me. I was getting real close to doing more with that dick, than just wipe it with a towel, and I wanted it, and I wanted it bad!

"Troy, I'm gonna lay down here on my back, and you get down there between my legs. I'm gonna just lay here and let you get used to it and let you go at it at your own speed. I know the idea of putting your mouth on some guy's dick is really gonna be pretty weird to you, but hey guy, remember you've already had your tongue up in my ass, so putting your mouth on my dick shouldn't be too much trouble now, should it?"

As I scooted up between Jack's legs, I looked up at him and answered, "I don't think putting my mouth on it's gonna be the big problem — it's gonna be if I can get it in my mouth! Seriously man, after last Tuesday and seeing that big thing, the next day I tried to stick a Coke can in my mouth to see if I could get it open that far, and I couldn't do it! You got one fucking big dick man, I hope like hell I can!"

Slowly I started at the bottom base of it, and started licking my way up on the bottom, and around to the top of it, and then up toward the tip of it. As I was licking, I was playing with some mighty big balls too. For some funny reason, hanging onto Jack's bag of nuts, and kinda pulling 'em down, for some funny reason just made it easier for me to control his dick. One hand was full of nuts, and the other hand was full of one damn big dick. Slowly I licked up and I finally I had my tongue on the head of that dick, and that head felt like I was starting to lick a golf ball or maybe a big lemon. I took a big, really big deep breath, and aimed my mouth for it! I was actually gonna be putting some man's cock in my mouth, and I wondered just why in the hell I didn't just keep trying to tell myself, "You can't do that! You can't suck on some other man's cock! You aren't supposed to suck on another man's cock!"

The more I told myself that, the hungrier I got for it! The more I wanted the whole fucking thing down in my throat. For almost my entire life, I knew that one man was never supposed to put another man's cock in his mouth, and right then, that was all I wanted to do! I wanted it and I needed that dick. I got right up on top of it, I got my mouth opened just as far as I could, and I pushed my face down, and to my shock, I took about two or three inches of it. My mouth was full — fucking full, but I really did have at least some of Jack's cock in my mouth!"

"Hey man, hey! Troy, Troy you're doing good man, you're doing good! Troy my man, I didn't expect you to take it that fast! I thought maybe I was gonna have to talk you into it man, but shit man, you were ready for it weren't you? I guess you really wanted that dick, didn't you?"

All I could do right then was wobble my head kinda up and down, trying to agree that, "Yes, I wanted it, I really did!" I couldn't tell Jack that I had wanted it ever since I laid out there in the park, and watched him get up and out of my ass, and then get dressed. When he stood there in the moonlight, putting his pants on that night, the whole site of that tremendous stick of meat hanging there, and then getting tucked back into his uniform pants was probably about the hottest scene that I had ever seen. The moon light that night, the muscles of his body, the shine of his skin, the size of his dick, and the whole idea that I had just been fucked by one hell of a hot black cop, and that enormous dick, was almost too much for me to control. And now, finally, I was on top of him, and it, and I was actually putting my mouth on his dick, and hopefully, maybe I was gonna be able to put most of it down in my throat!

"Hey Troy man! Let's do a little switching position here and get your mouth better lined up to take that thing. Flip up here, lay down on top of me so your face is facing my feet, and that way your throat and my dick will fit together better. My dick likes to aim up this direction when it's hard, and believe me man, right now it is fucking hard! So anyway, aimed in that direction, you can slide your mouth down on it better! So, flip over here man, get you mouth down there on my dick, and besides, with you laying that way, I'll have your ass right up here by my face, and I'll be able to eat out a little ass, chew on some nuts, or suck me a bunch of dick while you're doing my rod!"

I looked at Jack's enormous log, then looked at Jack's face and said, "Oh shit man, I hope I can take all of this thing — I do! Jack, right now it looks more like an oil tanker on a railroad instead of some guy's dick! I'm serious, man, I am!"

"Hey Troy guy, just lay down there and just let things happen. Come on man — you had some of it in your mouth a few minutes ago, so just do the same thing as you were doing down there, except this time, you'll be able to go down on it farther. Now get your ass up here by my face so I can chew on that ass and bite that little asshole of yours! Yeah man, yeah! Now just put your mouth down toward it and kinda of think of it as being some nice big cold fudge sickle like you had as a kid. I'm sure you put a whole one of those up in your mouth when you were a kid, didn't you?"

I tried to answer a, "Yeah," but part of me was kinda laughing from the thought comparing this big black piece of meat with a fudge sickle like I used to eat as a kid! All of a sudden I realized why I had liked those sickles so damn much as a little boy. It was my future, and I just did not know it! The other reason I couldn't answer Jack was — that yes — I did have his 'fudge sickle' as he called it, in my mouth, and my mouth was fucking full! And as much as I was sucking on it, none of it was melting like a fudge sickle does. It was getting bigger and bigger all of the time, not smaller and smaller!

As Jack pulled back a little from eating on my ass and my asshole, he laid his head back on the pillow and said, "Oh yes man, oh yes! Troy oh man, you are doing it, I can tell! You are on it and I can tell! Yeah man, do it, it feels good, it feels good! Suck it man, suck it and chew on it! Do it! Do it man, you are doing it! Troy, how much you got in your mouth man, how far down on it are you?"

Without pulling my mouth off of it — cause right then I was afraid that if I did, I wouldn't be able to get it back into my throat, I reached over and tried to show Jack that I thought I had about five or six inches of it in my mouth — by giving him a hand signal. I spread my fingers apart, to try and let him know that I thought maybe five or six inches of it.

"Keep it up guy, keep it up! You are doing good man, you are doing good! You suck on my cock man, and I'm gonna eat your ass out some more — yeah I am!"

And as soon as Jack got that stated, he immediately bit the edge of my asshole. Once again, it all went through my mind, 'Guys are not supposed to do this to each other! We are not — but we are — and it feels so damn good, why in the hell then, is it so wrong? Oh shit man, who in the hell cares, who cares? It's my mouth and his dick, and it's my ass and his mouth, and we both wanna do it, so who in the hell can say it's wrong? Nobody man — nobody!'

And with that thought, all of a sudden, I was eating the entire dick! The whole fucking thing! The entire length, all of it, and of course the full width of it too! All of a sudden I just simply threw my mouth down on it stronger and more forcefully, and even though it felt like it tore out the back of my throat, I took it! I had taken all of Jack's enormous, big, thick, black dick, and I was happy as hell! I wanted to pat myself on the back, and I guess maybe in a way, I did, cause Jack did it for me!

"Holy shit man, holy shit! Troy you OK man, you OK? What in the hell happened down there? Wow man, I will tell you that no man, no man has ever taken my dick like that! Troy, as many times as Bill has been on it, he still can't do that like you just did! Troy, you OK man, you OK?"

I pulled my head back up and off of that enormous thing, now bigger than what I thought earlier, and took a deep breath. I put both of my hands on the bed beside Jack's legs, steadied myself, took about three more deep breaths, just trying to get some air back into me, and then slowly and kinda of gently shook my head, and kinda said, "I did it, I did it! Jack, I ate the whole thing! I got my teeth down on the base of it man, I did! I don't know just how fucking far it went down inside of me, but man, I did it, I did it! Jack, I did it! I can't believe it, but I did it, and I didn't throw-up or choke! I did it!"

With my last, "I did it!" I collapsed completely down on top of Jack! I was exhausted, why I don't know, cause that whole thing only took about maybe two or three minutes, but all of a sudden, I was exhausted! Completely — totally — exhausted!

I was laying there with my ass right up by Jack's face and my legs on both sides of his head! He reached up and patted my ass and said, "Man, you are my trophy man, you are my trophy! Troy, you are number one on my page man, number one! Bill is good, he's real good, but I just found myself a new trophy. We gotta move here guy, my dick is stuck between us and I gotta get it moved."

With that comment, I did move and I got off of Jack, and then looked back at the stick of meat that I had just eaten to the depth of it, and said, Jack, I'm serious man, I can not believe I took all of that in my mouth and down my throat! I can't!"

"Well, believe me man, you did! Troy my man, you did! I could feel you hitting the base of it when all of a sudden, you slammed down on it like there was no tomorrow. What in the hell happened right then that made you do that?"

"Jack, all of a sudden, a lot of shit went through my mind, and all of a sudden I did not care what I had been told ever since I was a little kid! I had part of your dick in my mouth, and just all of a sudden, the hell with what everybody else thinks or says, I was living in glory, and I wanted it, and so I went for it! The hell with what other people say, I have decided I like dick, and I like dick up in my ass, and I like a dick down in my throat, and if nobody else likes it, the hell with them! It's my mouth and it's my ass, and I will put whatever I want in it, and let me tell you something Mr. Jack, it's gonna be your cock just as often as I can! I mean it man, I do! You got one hell of a big piece of equipment, but you now have a man that will take it anytime that you want to do it, and I mean it! Jack, I cannot believe how cutting though Cemetery Park the other night has changed my life, but it did! Jack, screw women, and I don't mean in the physical sense, I mean, screw 'em. Of all the time I was on the football field, grabbing guys, throwing 'em around, jumping down on top of 'em, watching 'em take showers and letting their dicks hang out, never did I really understand just why I liked football so fucking much! It wasn't the football, it was the guys and the guy-to-guy contact that I got out of it! Jack, I do not know how in the hell I was lucky enough to get you as my first guy, but thank God, I did!"

"You know what Troy — I kinda feel the same way about you! I told you that Bill is good in bed, or in the park, or wherever, but like I told you just a few minutes ago, I just found me a new trophy, with you! You are one hot fucker, and yeah, you've got a lot to learn, and a lot to experience, but man, if you are willing to let me do the stuff with you, then I kinda think that both of us can be feeling some pretty good feelings!"

As I looked up at Jack, since I was still laying the other direction on the bed, I almost yelled, "Hell yes man, hell yes, I am willing to work together with you! Shit man — hell yes!"

"Well, you know what the first thing is that we need to do, if we're gonna be working together?"

"What Jack, what?"

"Troy my man, you went down on me so fucking fast, I never got a chance to get my nuts off, and I'm still holding a major, major, hard on, and I'm gonna jerk it off, or if you want to, I'll let you. Which do you want?"

"Oh shit Jack, let me, let me!" I just about almost screamed when he asked me that!

Immediately I got out of the way, and got myself turned around so that I could get ahold of it, and I immediately started jerking it back and forth, back and forth! I never in my wildest dreams had ever thought that I'd have some man's dick in my hand, well actually in both hands, and that I would be jerking him off, and now look at what I was doing! I was actually jerking on a city policeman, one hell of a hot and hunky policeman, and one that has an eleven-inch long slonger on himself. I could not believe it — and I was the guy there, with my hands on it, and jerking on it!

Jack swung around on the edge of the bed, leaned back, rested on his hands back behind himself, and actually presented his dick and his balls to me as if a gift, so that I could use his manhood to my total and complete enjoyment! I grabbed ahold of that dick and I jerked it back and forth probably twenty or thirty times, when all of a sudden I heard Jack taking some really, really, deep breaths and I could tell he was just about to explode, and let everything fly! I knew from that night in the park that all hell was gonna come flying out of that dick, when he lets loose and shoots his wad!

"Oh Troy, oh Troy I'm about to cum man — I'm about to cumm! Oh shit man — oh shit! Oh Troy, I'm cummmmin man — I'm cummmmmin! Oh, shit man! Oh shit, that felt fucking good! Oh shit man — wow! Damn man — god alive, you know how in the hell, how to jerk a guy off don't you? Shit man, Troy, damn thanks man, thanks! When in the hell did you learn to do that?"

"Jack, I've never jerked off another guy! Never! That was the first time that I ever did that except to myself! That was my first time doing another guy! I guess I did OK — right?"

"Hell yes you did man, hell yes! Tell you what let's do! Come on, let's go in the shower and let me suck you off while we let the water run down on us? OK?"

All of a sudden nothing could have sounded better to me, nothing! I jumped up off of the bed, headed for the shower, got it turned on and kind of adjusted it as to the temperature, and as Jack stepped in, I started washing off the quart, or a quart and a half, of some of the thickest cum juices that I think a man can make. Of course, other than his, mine and Bill's, I never touched any other man's cum before, so I could be wrong, but when you think of the body that it comes out of, it's gotta be some pure gold cum. The better the container, the mixer and the operation of making it, has gotta make it some of the world's best! And here I was, rinsing it off of my chest, and down the drain. I actually felt guilty of doing that! I was wasting Jack's cum. Now what in the hell I was gonna do with it if I bottled it up, I had no idea, but still and yet — I still felt like I was throwing away something that should have been put in the safe.

Jack stepped in, watched me rinsing off his cum, and asked, "Not quite ready to take that and eat it yet, uh?"

All of a sudden I realized that maybe I was doing the wrong thing by not eating it! I just was not used to the idea of eating some other guy's juices, and honestly, I did not even think about that, until Jack mentioned it! Then I felt bad!"

Jack turned me around so that I was face to face with him, the water was running down off of the back of my head and hitting Jack on top of his head as he stooped down, right in front of my hardon, and then took it in his mouth. Feverishly he sucked on me and at the same time reached up and pinched both of my tits and just fucking turned me on to all extremes. I was getting a blowjob by the hottest looking cop on the force, and I was in another world! I grabbed ahold of Jack's head and really felt him pumping on my cock, both on my cock and by feeling his head moving back and forth! All of a sudden, I could not hold it any longer and I let out a yelling that I was gonna cum! "Oh Jack, Jack! Jack, I've gotta cum man, I've gotta!"

Jack just shook his head up and down, letting me know that he knew what I had said, and he was ready! I shot! I shot probably more in one shot than I had ever done before! Every time I am with this hunk of a master god of a man, I swear I shoot harder and harder than I ever have before.

Jack took my rod, pulled off of it, licked the sides of his mouth, licking the extra cum that was dripping out, and then licked all of the outside of my dick! I stood there, kinda leaning on the shower wall, and also still hanging onto Jack's head! I was in total heaven! Total!

As he finished up licking my rod clean, Jack then said, "Hey man, let's finish up here in the shower, I gotta hit the road. The only problem with you and me doing our thing together is that I always have a house I gotta head for, before it gets too late. Troy, you are one hell of a good guy to play with. Tonight is only going to be one of many, many — that is, if that's OK with you! OK with you?"

"Jack my man, that is one hell of a lot more than OK with me! You are the one person that I really, really wanna have sex with anymore! Bill, yeah, Bill too — but man — you are the man!"

Chapter Six

Middle of the Night

"Come on Bill, poke me man, poke me! Yeah man, yeah! Oh shit man, I'm so glad you came over here tonight! Man, that fucking rod of yours up in my ass always feels so fucking good! Come on man, keep it up, keep it up!"

It was late, like about 2:30 in the morning late, and I had gotten a very surprise visit from Officer Bill — one that I had not expected.

I told him, "Hit your cum man, come on, hit it and shoot it in me! Come on Bill, fuck me man, cause then I gotta suck on that rod of yours man, I gotta! You have gotten me so fucking horny showing up here all of a sudden tonight, I am about to go fucking crazy! Fuck me man, fuck me!"

"Hang on Troy, hang on! I'm cumin man, I'm cummmmmin! Oh shit man, oh shit! Damn man, I did it — I did it! Oh Troy my man — you got it — you got it! If you're gonna suck on me man, I don't think you're gonna get any juices out of it after that! Troy, it is fucking empty!"

"I don't care Bill, I don't! I need some dick in my mouth, and you are the man! With you and Jack both being out of town for a week and a half or whatever, to me it felt like a month! Seriously man, I need to suck on some dick! A few months ago, there is no way in hell that I would have ever told any guy that I'd even look at his dick, but man, you and Jack sure as hell have converted me! Hey, run into that bathroom and wipe my ass juices off of that dick and get back in here and let me suck on it! Bill, I need to do some sucking!"

Bill slipped into the bathroom and tidied up his all "juiced up" cock and returned back to the bed and laid down with his dick standing straight up in the air. I immediately opened my mouth and went down on it completely!

Just like when you are in the dentist chair — your mouth full of fingers and tools and the dentist insists on asking you questions, well that is what was now happening here with Bill and me. I had a big mouth full of cock, but yet Bill was asking me all kinds of questions, trying to figure out just why I was so out rigorously horny this night.

"Troy, I know Jack and I were out of town for a few days, but weren't you getting any sucking someplace else?

I shook my head, "No."

"Aren't you playing around with any other guys?"

Again, I shook my head, "No."

"Well, what about your gal, Shirley? Aren't you getting any from her lately?"

All of a sudden I pulled off of Bill's cock, looked up at him and said, "You and Jack are they only guys that I'm sucking on, or getting sucked by, or fucking, or getting fucked by, and Shirley and I broke up! Bill — doing this with you and Jack made me loose all interest in doing her anymore, and everything went straight down hill! She don't know what changed, but she does know that something changed, and she told me to fly a kite and to get the hell out of her life! So Bill, no — I'm not getting any sex from her — but I don't care! She doesn't have a dick like this for me to stick in my mouth and suck on — so I don't care anymore! But with you and Jack both being gone at the same time — that put me in a real bind! Now let me suck on this thing before it gets all old and limp! OK?"

I went back to sucking on Bill's rod, and Bill understood that maybe he needed to just lay there and let me go to it, for as long as I needed to do it!

Twenty minutes on Bill's dick, then another twenty or twenty five minutes licking everything, chewing on everything, sucking on everything, and just plain making love to every part of Bill's body, I then finally rolled over on the bed beside Bill. I then said, "Bill, don't you and Jack ever leave town at the same time again! I don't care what type of some important cop's meeting it is or what convention it is, you tell your captain or whoever schedules you guys for that stuff, that you two have got this horny guy here in town, that just plain needs at least one of you here, all of the time! Seriously man, for the entire time that you two were out of town, I did more street driving, looking for some lonely looking little guy that I thought needed it up in the ass, than I think most guys do in a lifetime! Seriously man, I was horny, horny, horny!"

"Shit man, I guess I'm sorry about you and Shirley, but if that's the best, then I guess it's OK, but I do know that I'm really sorry we didn't set you up with a good cop substitute to use while we were gone. Hey man, I just did not realize how fast you got so horny! Troy, it's only been what, three months since that first time in Cemetery Park? You converted over to the gay stuff fast didn't you?"

"Yes, I guess I did! Bill, every since that night in Cemetery Park, I've been in bed with either you or Jack at least three or four times a week, and going for a week and a half, or two weeks, or whatever it was, that was a bitch! A fucking bitch! I just plain know that since you guys got me started with all of the sucking and fucking, I need it all of the time, I mean — a lot! You mentioned that you were sorry you didn't set me up with a good substitute cop to use while you were gone, you serious? Are you serious — you mean that?"

"Well yeah, I guess maybe I am. Yeah Troy, if I had known that you weren't getting any from Shirley anymore, I could have set you up with Kenny. He's kinda new in our precinct and Jack and I just found out, like about two or three days before the convention, that Kenny is one of the more, open gay officers we have on staff. They moved him over to our area so that we'd have an openly gay cop to deal with some of the stuff at the gay bars, and yeah, probably at the gay bath house!"

"So tell me, tell me, about this Kenny guy! He knows you play around with guys? Does he know Jack plays around?"

"On a very, very, confidential basis, yes he does. When they brought him into our precinct, they asked all of us to be honest and open with Kenny if any of us knew anything about the gay community or any of the people in the gay community. We were to meet with him very confidentially, out of the office, and share whatever we could, and everything was sworn to secrecy, so that anybody that knew anything, would go talk to him. So anyway, yeah Jack and I did talk to him, and he knows we are married guys and that yes, we do play around, but we trust him fully! He's really helped a couple of the other areas a lot, and that's why we now have him here. So anyway, yeah, I could have told him about you and seen if he could have stepped in for a day or two, or maybe I should have said, a night or two!"

"So tell me about him, what's he like? Tell me!"

All of a sudden Bill's cell phone started ringing, and in shock, Bill looked at me and said, "What in the hell! Who in the hell is calling me now?"

Jumping up off of the bed and grabbing his phone, he quickly looked at it and then looking at me and said, "It's Jack! It's Jack!"

"Hello! What in the hell is up man, — what's up? Yeah — yeah — yes — ya — OK — yeah, yeah I just got out of his ass and for about an hour he's been all over me sucking and chewing. Jack, we screwed up on not getting him somebody to take care of, or somebody to take care of him, while we were in Tampa! He and Shirley broke up — no, I didn't know that — and anyway he admitted he went driving around, just trying to find some ass to poke, but I guess didn't do any good! Yeah, hell yes — OK, OK, yeah OK! OK bye!"

Standing there and looking at me, Bill then said, "Guess what! Jack's in the parking lot. He drove by looking for my bike since it wasn't at the station, and he decided maybe he'd better call me before he just came up to the apartment. He's on his way up! That's OK — I hope! I mean — it is OK if he comes up, right?"

"Holy crapping shit yes! Hell yes! My God man, I can't believe this! Like two weeks, without either one of you guys, and now, all of a sudden in the middle of the night, you're both here! He is gonna plan on getting naked and doing some good stuff, ain't he?"

"I'm sure he is, but he did forewarn me that he can't stay very long. He just got off shift, and his wife will be expecting him to come in before it gets too much later, so I'm not sure how long he can be here. I'm the lucky one — Martha is out of town herself till Friday night, so I haven't seen her since before I left. But hey, who cares! She's gone, and I get to be here with one horny guy! Couldn't be better! Oh hey — be right back! I think Jack just tapped on the front door!"

Jack and Bill returned back to the bedroom. Jack was leading Bill by grabbing onto his rod, and rather pulling him forward.

Looking at me, all stretched out on the bed, Jack just made one statement. "Roll over man, I haven't had me any good sweet tight ass for about two weeks now, and I need it bad!"

Bill looked at him and asked, "Well hell man, what about me?"

Looking at Bill as he stripped, he just replied, "Oh hell man — you don't count!"

Jack stripped everything off, completely! His entire uniform seemed to come off much more quickly, to me anyway, than I had ever seen it come off before.

Jack stooped down, grabbed Bill's cock and threw it in his mouth for only about five seconds, then told Bill to get up by my head, "I wanna suck on that rod, while I stuff my ole rod up in this sweet little ole ass laying here!"

I was stretched out on the bed, on my gut, and my hands stretched out above his head. Bill got in position right above my head, Jack mounted the bed, then after a very quick squeeze of the KY lube, and onto his dick and into my ass, he dropped down and went in! I jumped slightly, but gave no negative comment about taking the entire black dick up and into my ass, as I thought — finally — and again! I had been very anxious for this to happen, I just didn't know it was gonna happen in the middle of the night!

Sucking on Bill's rod, and fucking my ass, it only took about two minutes total, before Jack was letting both of us know, "Oh shit men, oh shit! I'm gonna cum guys — I'm gonna cum! Oh Troy, hang on man, hang on, it's gonna hit you man, it's gonna come fucking flying out, it's — oh shit man — I'm cummmin — I'm cummmmmmmin! Oh man, oh man! Oh shit that felt good! Man, I just can't go for like a week and a half or two weeks or whatever, without some of your good tight gay ass! Damn man, damn! Hey Troy ole guy, you OK? You OK?"

Laying there now with Bill virtually sitting down on my head, and Jack sprawling out along my back, I simply said, "I'm in heaven man, I'm in fucking heaven! I'm more than OK — I am fucking OK."

Jack slightly moved off of me, and Bill positioned himself so that he was straddled my head, and I stated. "Oh shit men, oh shit! Do you guys know that this is only the second time that I've been fucked by both of you guys on the same night! Wow, oh shit! I've got so much cop cum up in my ass tonight, it's like nobody's business! Oh shit man, oh shit! God, that was great! I can't believe that my playmates are both hot, body building type of married cops! I can't believe it! Just think of how many gay guys would love to have just one hot cop fucking his ass, and I've got me two, and two of the hottest fucking cops anywhere! Thanks guys, thanks for doing me and making me feel so fucking good!"

Jack stood up, went into the bathroom and rather tidied himself up some, came back into the bedroom and said, "Guys, I am really sorry, but I gotta get home. I sure as hell did not expect to do this tonight, but when I finally found your bike down there Bill, I knew stuff was happening up here, and I sure as hell did not want to be left out! Bill, you staying here the rest of the night?"

All of a sudden, I entered in with a, "Hell yes he is! I did not know until just a few minutes ago that his wife is out of town till Friday, so yeah he's staying, tonight, maybe tomorrow night and maybe till Friday if I can get him to do it! You guys ran out of town on me for that stupid meeting, and now I gotta make up for lost time and lost dick!"

Bill looked at Jack as Jack was getting presentable again and just simply said, "Oh, I didn't know that, but I guess the orders have been stated, right?"

Jack buckled up his belt buckle, looked at Bill and simply said, "Sounds like it, sounds like it! Hey guys gotta go, gotta go!"

I emphatically told Jack, "Thank you," about three times, and as Bill walked with Jack to the front door, he did mention that when the call came in, he was in the process of telling me about Kenny, since he had stated that maybe they should have set me up with a substitute while they were out of town.

With the mention of Kenny's name, Jack immediately turned toward Bill and asked, "Oh shit man, have you seen the dick on that guy yet? Holy crap man! Us black guys are gonna have to start pulling our dicks out a little longer, if many more white guys show up with dicks like his! Hey, us black guys like to know we're the ones with the big long dicks, but shit man, I saw his one day in the restroom, and shit man, it's big! That was after he and I had our little chat, so he sure did not have any problem of pulling it out and letting me see it! I'm gonna get on that one some day, believe you me! Hey, gotta go, see you tomorrow!"

Jack left the apartment, Bill returned back to the bedroom and asked, "So, I guess I'm supposed to stay here tonight — right?"

Scooting over some to give Bill some space in the bed, I told him, "Hell yes! And now — back to that Kenny guy! I just heard what Jack said about him! Have you seen it yet? What's my chances of getting him over here? Any idea?"

"No, I haven't seen it yet! But sure does sound like something that we all need to see, don't it?"

"From what I'm hearing, I'd say so! Do you have any idea if he's got a partner or not?"

"I have no idea, no idea at all. Why, you interested? You looking for a man already, or is it just the talk of how fucking big his dick is that's getting you all turned on?"

"Hey man, a cop? Hell yes! I'd go for having me a cop for a partner, and hey man, if he's got a big dick, that makes it that much better! We gotta see if I can meet him sometime, OK?"

"OK, yeah, we will. Let me talk to him and let him know that I've got one horny, ass hungry, and stiff dick friend that would like to meet him if at all possible, and we'll see what I can do. But, for now, know what's gonna happen?"

"Yeah, yeah, I do! I'm gonna get my ass fucked some more, right? Gonna fuck this hungry ass some more — please?"

"Roll over man, roll over, we're running out of night time, we gotta do this so we can get at least an hour or two of sleep! Give it to me — give it to me! I wanna kiss it and then I wanna fuck it! Come on man, give me your ass!"

Chapter Seven

What You Up to Lately?

"Well, hello Scotty, how in the hell are you? I have not seen you in years!"

Totally unexpected, Bradley Scott, Bill's son, came walking into the shop and stuck his hand out to meet and greet me.

"Yeah, I know man, I know. Once in awhile we just don't do the stuff that we should, and not staying in contact with you, I think is one of 'em. How you doing?"

"Pretty good Scotty, I guess pretty good! How you doing? What's up man, what you up to lately?"

"Hey just the normal, I guess, just the normal. Working for Barston National Trucking in their office, doing the scheduling stuff! I heard the other day, that you had the shop here, and so I decided that just maybe I oughta stop by and say 'Hi." How long you had it?"

"It'll be three years shortly. When I first got it, did everything all by myself, but thankfully things did go good enough to where I've got Jimmy here now helping me out! So anyway, things are kinda OK. What about you? You and Janet still together, or did you guys finally get married, and me just not knowing it?"

"Oh no! No, Janet and I broke up about a year out of school, and I'm still on the single scene. I've gone through a whole bunch of gals, but for some reason or another, they just don't end up being what I guess I'm looking for. You? What about you? You married now?"

"No — as you put it — still on the single scene. After getting out of school I had a gal by the name of Shirley for quite awhile, but then we went our separate ways, and I'm still the old bachelor guy! Hey, how about a beer? Jimmy's here, and I don't think stuff is gonna get any busier than it is right now, and so, anyway, if you want a beer I can just let Jimmy take care of the place and then let him close up — what do you say?"

"Yeah, hell yeah, if you can, yeah!"

I went to the back for a few minutes and told Jimmy that I and Scotty, an old time friend that had stopped in, were gonna go over to the Brick Pub and grab a couple of beers, so if anything came up that he needed to talk to me about, give me a call on my cell phone.

I and Scotty decided to take separate cars, since after the drinks we'd be headed different directions.

After going in and taking a couple of places at one of the tables, the bartender delivered the beers and I then asked Scotty, "Hey man, tell me. How'd you happen to hear that I've got the shop? Somebody tell you?"

Leaning in closer onto the table, Scotty looked over at me and quietly said, "Troy, I saw you over at the Cattle Barn about a week ago."

I put a very quizzed expression on my face and asked, "The Cattle Barn?"

"Yes Troy, let's not play games here! You know the Cattle Barn, and I do too! I saw you in there last Friday night, and yes, I admit, I avoided you. I wasn't sure how to handle it. I told the guy that I was with that I knew you, but it had been years since I had seen you, and I did not know that you hung out in gay bars. He told me that all he knew about you was that you had just kinda recently been coming in there, but he did know you had a auto repair shop over on 12th at about Valley Road. Troy, I saw who you left with! Hot looking stud, about 27 or 28, taller than you, and had a red shirt on. Troy, I saw you put your hand on his butt! Don't deny it man, I was there too."

Sitting there completely shocked, rather stunned, rather speechless, I did finally ask, "Why were you in there?"

Leaning in closer yet, Scotty simply said, "I'm gay! Troy, I'm gay and I know you are too! A man does not go into a gay bar, be as friendly as you were with that guy that night, put your hand on his ass, as you are walking out, and not be gay! Right?"

In complete shock, not now really knowing just how to handle everything, especially since I knew I simply could not talk about Bill being one of my major playmates, I simply kinda said, "Yeah." And I then said nothing.

"Come on man, loosen up! There is nothing wrong! Yes, I'm gay, I admit it, and I just happened to find out that you are too, but I just did not know that until, like last week. When I decided that I did want to talk to you about it, well about life in general, that's when I decided to drive over to 12th Street and see what repair shops were around there. I went into Valley River Repair first, and when you weren't there, I just told the guy there who I was looking for, that we were old high school classmates, and he told me which shop was yours. That's how I found you! Relax man, relax! Nothing wrong here man, nothing. Well, except for maybe we're in the wrong bar. Wanna go over to the Cattle Barn?"

Without really saying anything, I very silently utter a, "Yeah," and shook my head, "Yes."

We finished the beers that we already had, then simply got up, walked out of the bar, and as I was getting into my car, Scotty did ask! "Now you are gonna show up there right? I mean you're not gonna go running out on me are you?"

I looked at Scotty and replied, "Uh, yeah. I'll be there Scotty, I'll be there."

Quietly we each got in our respective cars, well in my case, my Jeep, and drove the three miles over to the Cattle Barn Bar.

Once inside, we found a booth that was rather out of the way, but still in good view of the other patrons.

Each with a beer in our hands, Scotty quietly looked at me and said, "I know man, I know. You thought it was all hidden from everybody you know, didn't you? We all do! Hey, it just happened that you and I ended up here, on the same night. No big deal! I know I should have talked to you that night, but yeah, it was a surprise to see you in here, so I was kind of dumb struck. How long you been gay? Well, I don't mean how long, we all are our whole lives, but what I mean is how long have you been out?"

Still stunned and shocked, I was silently trying to figure out just how I was gonna discuss this without telling Scotty that it's his dad that moved me into the gay scene. Mentally, I thought, "Tell him stuff, but keep the idea of police officers out of it, yeah — no cop talk! Make it be other guys."

"Uhhh, Scotty, just real recently. Just a few months. Things between me and Shirley weren't going so good, and one night I just happened to run across two guys doing it out in Cemetery Park, and it got me all turned on, and I found out I liked it, and so, anyway, that's what happened."

"Out in Cemetery Park? I didn't know that was gay play spot! Cemetery Park?"

"No, no! No, it's not. One night I was taking a short cut home, and anyway, these two guys were in there doing it, and I hid for a while until I got such a hard-on, that I finally told 'em I wanted to do it too. Anyway, that was my first time."

"So do you and those guys still get together? You done it with them anymore?"

Mentally, I was screaming at myself, "I'm gonna lie, I know I'm gonna lie, I've got to, I can't tell him who it was, I gotta lie."

"Un no! Just that once. But they told me about this bar, and so I find guys in here once in awhile to do stuff with. Like that guy last week. I don't even remember his name. But he sucked me and I sucked him, and that was all. How long you been doing stuff?"

"Hey man, a long time! Remember that night when you and I did those two chicks from over at Citywide? That was my last time with some gal! Troy, I will be honest with you and tell you that I was one hell of a lot more interested in looking at your dick than I was in either one of those girls. Man, if I had only known then what I know today. I'd have been doing you right then and there instead of trying to act like I wanted either one of them. Hell man, maybe that would have opened you up to this stuff a hell of a lot earlier!

"Yeah maybe so, who knows. So Scotty, you live alone or have a lover or what?"

"Well, yeah I live alone but not by choice! I've had a couple of relationships, but nothing good and strong. What about you? Now that you kinda know who you really are a little more, you gonna try and find yourself a man?"

"God man, I don't know! I haven't even thought about that!"

"So tell me, what kind of guys are you going for? What type of guys have you been playing with?"

"Oh just kinda like the guy I left here with — the one that you saw. I guess I gotta admit, I like the more athletic kind. Guys that are in good shape."

"So — what about me? Am I in shape enough? Can we do it? I'd love to take you to bed Troy! Like I told you about that night with those girls, I would have done you in a second if had thought I could have. Come on, let's go to my place please! Please, can we?"

Looking at Scotty, and remembering the size of dick that I remembered Scotty having, I just looked at him, and said, "Yeah man, yeah!"

One quick ride later, one quick grab of a beer from the frig, and one quick strip of the clothes, I and Scotty were finally, after many years of knowing what the other guy was hanging, were finally in bed and finally doing something exciting — sexually exciting — together. The two former football players that used to throw guys around on the field, were now in bed, and throwing each other around in the bed.

"Shit Scotty, I remember seeing this rod of yours while in school, and then of course that last night with the Citywide girls, it is big man — big! Push it in me and fuck the hell out of me man, fuck me! Fuck me with it man — fuck me — it feels so damn good up in there! Damn man, I wish we had been doing this a long time ago. It feels so fucking good, it does!"

As Scotty was up on my back, and fucking the hell out of my ass, he replied, "Shit yes man, shit yes! Of all of the queeny little guys that I have fucked, to think that all I would have needed to do was give you a call and then I could have been laying up here on top of this muscled body, poking this tight ass instead of doing those poor little sorry asses. Damn Troy, wish I had known about you one hell of a lot earlier!"

"But Scotty, ya gotta remember. I just got into this real recently! If you'd have called me just a few months ago, I'd have hung up on you and probably told you to go to hell in a breadbasket man! I'd have told you to go straight to hell, just as I hung up the phone!"

"I know it man, I do! Troy, what I wanna know is just who in the hell that was, that night in the park, that was so fucking good that it made you decide that night that you really did like gay sex better than straight sex? Who in the hell was that Troy? Who did you play with?"

"Hey Scotty, like I said, just a couple of guys! Don't know who they were. Guess I was too ashamed to even tell them who I was. Don't worry about it. I don't know!"

Attempting to get Scotty off of that line of questioning, I then rather quickly told him that I was wanting to do some fucking too, and was he about ready to let his jazz juices fly, so that we could change spots.

"Hang tight Troy, hang tight! I'm getting really close man, I'm getting really close, oh man, oh shit man, here it comes Troy, it's coming man it's coming! Troy, oh Troy I'm cumin man — oh I'm cummmmmin! Oh shit man, oh shit — I just gave you one fucking ass full! Hey guy, if you're gonna fuck me too, you gotta give me a couple of minutes to re-coop here! I am fucking beat man, fucking beat! You have got one hell of a hot ass to fuck man, you have! Somebody taught you how in the hell to squeeze that ass when a dick is up in there, that is for sure! "

After a few minutes of rest and re-coop, Scotty put his ass in the air and told me, his new fuck buddy, to — "Go for it man! Go for it! It's been about four or five days since I've had me a real man up in there, so fuck the hell out of me man — fuck the hell out of me! Let me feel that dick up in me, give it to me, give it to me hard!"

I obeyed orders! I fucked the hell out of Scotty, actually for two reasons. Number one — Scotty's ass felt good — damn good, and number two — I did not want Scotty to have any more opportunity and to say or ask anything about the guys that I had been playing with. I did not want any more questions! I decided that we just needed to keep that subject off of the table, so to say. My main problem right then, was trying to figure out how to tell Jack that I and Scotty were now doing the sex thing together, and knowing that Jack had already told me that if I ever do anything with Scotty, he wanted to be involved. I had no idea of how I was going to handle this! I just knew though, that sex with Scotty was way too much fun to let it go by the wayside, but how in the world was I gonna handle it with Jack, and then of course, Bill, I had no idea!

Chapter Eight

You Don't Wanna Know, Do Ya?"

Jack had just stopped into the shop to talk to me as per my cell phone call a few minutes earlier. I did intend — and I emphasize the word intend — to tell Jack about my night, last night with Scotty, but low and behold, just as Jack got there and we did some of the usual — whenever in a position to do it — cock grabbing and feeling, I looked out the front window and almost exploded, "Oh shit Jack! Jack, Scotty is coming in. Bill's Scotty is coming in! We can't let him know we know each other — well, like we really do! Play like a customer! Here he comes!"

As Scotty came in the front door, I looked at him and greeted him in a rather normal fashion.

Officer Jack looked at Scotty and said, "Hey, I think I know you, don't I? Are you Officer Bill Scott's son?"

Looking at the officer, Scotty did reply, "Yes — yes I am. You're Officer Jack Tainer, right? Is that right?"

"Yes it is, yes — you're right? I remember you from — well, like years ago coming to precinct parties with your Mom and Dad. How you doing?"

"Doing good, I guess! Well, as far as I can tell! Hey guys, I didn't mean to interrupt anything here, I'm sorry."

Quickly I responded with, "Oh that's OK Scotty. Officer Tainer was just inquiring about when he could bring his Jeep in for a tune up. That's all."

Then looking at Scotty, Officer Tainer excused himself, said he had to get back on the beat, and told Troy that he'd bring the Jeep in next Monday! He then told Scotty that he was glad to see him again, and told me, "Thanks! I'll see you Monday morning." And, with all of those lies now on the table, he left the shop.

As Officer Tainer, or Jack, left the shop, I could definitely see some facial expression of confusion on Jack's face as well as somewhat of a questioning "handshake" as he left. He was leaving, very confused — but nonetheless — leaving. He got in his cruiser, tried to look back toward me, but did not have a clear line of sight. He drove off.

Inside of the shop, I said, "Well Scotty, I really did not expect to see you in here today. How you doing today?"

Looking around as he entered the shop office, just to see who else was around, Scotty replied, "OK, doing OK. We here by ourselves?"

"Yeah Scotty, yeah. I gave Jimmy the afternoon off — so yeah — just you and me. So how you doing today, OK?"

"Oh hell yeah man, hell yes! I thought I'd just stop in to tell you face to face that I really, really enjoyed that, last night, but now I've got one hell of a big question! Troy, how in the hell do you know officer Jack? How do you know him?"

"Hey Scotty, I don't know — think he just stopped in here one day to inquire about something for his Jeep. Yeah, yeah, that's how we met.

"Come on Troy, that's a fucking lie! I know it is! How do you know him? He fucking stood there the entire time we were talking and he kept looking at my crotch! Yes, hell yes I was looking at his too, but for some funny reason he was more fucking interested in my crotch than anything any of us were talking about! Troy, tell me, how in the hell do you know officer Jack? Are you guys playing around? Are you and Jack fucking each other? Come on man, come on! I saw the way he grinned at you and then kinda looked down a couple of times. Come on tell me, tell me!"

After about four or five more minutes of some very serious questioning about just how did I happen to know Officer Tainer, and every explanation that I tried to "make-up" rather fell to the wind, I finally admitted.

"Scotty, Jack was one of the two that I found doing their thing out in Cemetery Park that night! Yes, Jack and I do fuck around cause he was one of the original guys that I saw doing the thing, and I went over to 'em and told 'em I wanted to join. Yes, Jack and I fuck each other."

"Oh my God man, oh my God! And Troy, I have lusted and lusted over that guy, wanting to get into his pants for years and years now! He's on the force with Dad and one day I saw him in a pair of really hot looking Speedos at a big precinct pool party, and he was showing everything! I mean man, if it wasn't everything, then I don't know how much that guy has got stuck up in there! You know — now that I think about it — I think he was kinda looking at my crotch that day too, but hell, I was there with Mom and Dad and everybody else from the precinct and all their families — yes, including Jack's family, so if he was wanting to say or do anything, there was no way in hell he could! Damn man, damn, now I really am wondering if maybe he was checking me out! I know one thing for sure, I sure as hell was checking him out, and have dreamt about wanting to see all of him — all naked — all bare, and —all hanging out, ever since. Troy, he was only one of two — who in the hell was the other guy? Who was he playing with? Who'd he have?"

"Hey Scotty, I don't know, ('lie, lie, lie, I am lying like crazy here') Scotty, I don't know. I and Jack did some stuff but I don't know who the other guy was."

"The hell you don't Troy! I can tell from the look on your face that you do! Is it someone that I know? Troy, tell me, is it someone that I know? Somebody else from the school? Who? Who was it?"

"Scotty, don't ask, please! You aren't gonna wanna know, seriously man, you just don't wanna know!"

"I don't want to know!!?? Why in the hell wouldn't I want to know? Troy — Troy — what are you saying man? What in the hell are you saying? Troy, look at me man, look at me! Troy — my Dad? Was the other guy my Dad? Are you and my Dad fucking around together? Troy — Troy, I'm asking man, I'm asking — is it my Dad?"

"Scotty, what if it was? You don't wanna know if it was or was not your Dad — do ya? You don't wanna know, do ya?"

"Yes, I do! Yes, I do! Troy, I have wondered about him for a long time now! Yeah, he and Jack work together, and yeah, whenever there is some out of town type of meeting, they always seem to get to go together. That pool party I told you about earlier, yeah my Dad was looking at that pair of Speedos on Jack as much as I was, and I think some of the other officers too. When I was still living at home, there were way too many nights that he "just did not get home as quickly as he had originally said he would," even for a policeman. Back then, I wondered just what in the hell he was doing, and since I was looking at hot cops then too, I wondered. Now I know! He was fucking and getting fucked by some of those hot cops that I was licking my chops over! And yes Troy, — he's a motorcycle patrolman, and yes, those damn tight uniform pants those guys wear, are damn hot on their asses! Yes, I know, I've been checking all of 'em out for years! I just never got a chance to fuck around with any of 'em, and now I find out you've been doing my Dad! Damn man! Damn! Troy, you gotta get me set up with Jack! I want that man and I want that man in my ass! I have wanted that man for years, but was too fucking afraid to try anything cause of him and Dad being friends. Shit man, if I had only known! Troy, how fucking big is his dick? It has got to be one fucking big log, right? I mean man, it shows — just like it did today, even though he's got pants on and not Speedos — it shows like a light bulb! Really more like a fucking long fluorescent tube. Hell it looks like it's about that long! Oh shit man, I want him. Come on man, you gotta get me set up with him!"

"Scotty! I understand about you being all excited about Jack being a playmate, but what about your Dad? You just found out that your Dad plays with guys too! You shook? —You shocked? —What're you feeling about that? You OK with that?"

"Hell yeah man, I'm OK. I'm just more disappointed that I never knew about Jack! Jack and Dad do play around together all the time, I assume, right? Is that right?"

"Yeah, yeah they do. I kinda guess they were trying to find a steady third guy, the night I happened on 'em. They kinda took me under their arm, so to say, and really taught me the stuff. Seriously man, Jack and your Dad are the first guys that I had ever done anything with, and they're the ones that rather taught me all the ropes, so to say."

"Shit man! So you been fucking around with my old man, and big man Jack, and I'm the guy that's been wanting to get in bed with either one of 'em for years, but yet — you're the one that gets both of 'em for your very first gay sex! Damn, life just ain't fucking fair!"

"Uhh, in bed with either one of 'em? Is that what you said?"

"Yeah, why? Yeah!"

"You wanna go to bed with your Dad? Is that what you're saying?"

"Yeah, yeah! Hell yeah man — I don't have a problem with that! Hell, I'd love to be in bed with him and Jack all at the same time! Well — come to think of it, I guess maybe you've already done that — right?"

"Well, yeah, yeah, a number of times. Yeah."

"Fucking shit man, fucking shit! Life is not fair! Troy, is Dad fun in bed? Does he fuck good? His dick's not as big as Jack's is it? It can't be! Dad's a white guy, Jack's a big black man, his dick's gotta be one hell of a lot bigger, right?"

"Yeah, yeah, but your Dad fucks good. He does man, he does. He fucked me the very first time I did anything, that night out in Cemetery Park! Yeah man, yeah, he fucks good! Why Scotty? Scotty, you wanting to get fucked by your Dad? You want that?"

"Yeah Troy, yeah, but — I want fucked by Jack first! I've lusted over what I know damn well is in that crotch and I want it and I want it bad! Damn man, what in the hell does it feel like to get that much meat pushed up in your ass? Come on Troy, come on! I am sure he is toting more meat and probably bigger balls in that crotch than any guy's, I've ever been with! Damn man — shit — I still cannot believe it that you have only been playing with guys for what, three months, and you've been fucked by, and have fucked, what I think is the hottest fucking cop in this state and probably all the states around it! Shit man, shit! OK, now time to figure out some stuff here. OK?"

I looked at Scotty and answered, "OK! But like what? What are we gonna figure out here man, what are you talking about?"

"Getting me and big Jack together! What in the hell do you think I'm talking about? I want that dick of his up in my ass, and I need you to help me get it! OK?"

"Scotty, I'm not so worried about getting you and Jack together, I'm more worried about what your Dad is gonna think and say when he finds out that you now know he does the guy stuff."

"Not so worried about getting me and Jack together? Why not? Why'd you say that? What does that mean?"

"Scotty, your Dad knows I know you! Jack knows I know you! One day I asked your Dad if he's seen your dick lately. He said no, but then wanted to know if you and I had played around together and I of course said, "No," but Jack then told me that if I ever got a chance with you that I was to get him involved, cause he saw what your crotch looked like in those Speedos that day at the pool, and he's wanted to play with it ever since. Scotty, that's what I was gonna tell Jack today when you walked in. He does not know about last night yet. That was what I asked him to stop in here for today. That's one of the reasons that I gave Jimmy the afternoon off. To rather, pay back some extra time, that he's put in. Him just happening, to not be here this afternoon, was pre-planned. I thought I was gonna have a talk with Jack and tell all about what happened last night, and that yeah, you and I had now done it, but, when all of a sudden you drove in, it stopped everything. I know damn well right now that Jack is totally confused as to just how did you happen to show up here today, after you and I had not seen each other for years! I'm sure he is confused as hell about just what is happening. And yes, did you notice he kept looking at your crotch? He's still wanting that dick, I know he is! He's already told me that!"

"Troy, I can't believe it man, I can not! I am so fucking glad that we happened in at the Cattle Barn at the same time that night. Without that, we might have never found out about each other. I know, I should have talked to you that night, but then, I saw you feeling up the ass on that hot stud you left with, so I guess maybe things worked out better this way. I have now found out about Officer Tainer and my Dad too. And after last night, I will say that for a guy that just got started — or so you say anyway — you sure as hell can take a big dick up in your ass easily! I mean man, my dick is not the smallest in the world, and yeah, not the biggest either, but Troy, I will tell you that you took my tool one hell of a lot faster than most guys do! You did good! Should I assume that big black Officer Jack, is the one that taught your ass how to open so nice and quickly? I know damn well that dick of his has got to feel fucking good going up inside of your ass, right? Damn man, I am so fucking jealous! I am!"

"Yeah, yeah! Jack's big thing is what got my ass to know that it needs to open fast, but Scotty — your Dad's dick feels pretty fucking good in there too! It's no little squatty one either. Honestly man, I know where you got your dick size from! So if you wanna see what it feels like to get fucked by you — let your Dad do it, it's a damn nice dick too! Maybe not black, but then, you can't feel color anyway!"

Chapter Nine

"What Did You Just Say!?"

"Hey Kenny, what's up man, what's up?

"Oh hi Jack! How you doing?"

"Well, I'm doing okay, but what in the hell are you doing in here at this time? This is kinda late for you to be in here doing paper work, isn't it?"

"Oh! Oh yeah, maybe so. Kinda making up some time that I kinda took off yesterday. I left kinda earlier than I should have and so I'm making up for it now. Don't say anything to the Captain, okay?"

"Yeah, OK, but what happened that you took off early yesterday. Something happen at home? Everything OK?"

Kenny then said, "No, no, everything there is OK, it's OK."

Then looking around the station to be sure nobody was close by and could over hear, Kenny rather leaned over toward Jack a little more closely and softly said, "Your man Troy! Hot little fucker ain't he?"

Looking at Kenny with a very shocked expression on his face to go along with the total state of confusion, Jack rather quickly asked, "Troy!? Troy, what are you talking about, what are you saying?"

"Ended up over at Troy's place last night. Shit man, does he fuck! I mean man, does he ever!"

Looking closely at Kenny and also leaning in a little closer, Jack asked, "What!? You did what? How in the hell did that happen? What?"

"Well, kinda like this. Bill and I were out doing some surveillance, of just checking out some areas that some of the guys use, and when we drove past Troy's shop, Bill mentioned to me that was the shop he owned. He explained the who "he" was by letting me know he was talking about the guy that you and he had told me you two were kinda using whenever possible. The guy that you guys found in Cemetery Park that night."

"Kenny, what in the hell happened? You guys drove by, so how did that get you and Troy together? I don't understand."

"Well, I kinda guess maybe I just did a little extra surveillance, and after we got back to the station I made some rather lame excuses for taking the rest of the shift off, and I took my F-150 over to see if maybe I could get a fast lube on it, and of course also get a good glimpse of the guy you two had been playing with."

"And —?"

"I ran home and changed clothes first! I wanted to do that so that he didn't know I was part of the force, and then went over there and just played like a normal customer. I've got a pair of tight Levi's that fit me to a "T" and I will admit, that ass of those Levi's, shows off my ass better than any other pair of pants I got, so I put 'em on — wanting my ass to look really hot and good! I put on a sleeveless white t-shirt that, yes, I will admit, makes my upper half look kinda like something out of some muscle magazine. I tried my damndest to look as hot as I could! You and Bill had already told me how fucking hot Troy is, and I wanted him to look at me and lust! And I think he did! He kept it pretty normal — business normal — but yeah, I saw him glance down toward my crotch when I walked in. I didn't have it all tucked back in and under. I wanted some of it to show, and I guess maybe I did it right. I glanced at myself in a window reflection as I walked up to the building, and hell yes man — my crotch even turned me on some! Looked damn good to me!"

Once again looking around to make sure nobody was standing too close, Jack again asked, "And, yeah — so what happened?"

"Well, I just went in, asked him if he could do a quick lube on the truck, and he said, 'Yeah, sure can! Pull it in and let me get to it!' So I did, and he started getting to work on it and I just kinda stood there and acted like real normal. I asked him stupid stuff like, like how long had he had the shop, did he work there alone — since I did not see anybody else around, found out later that his helper, the Jimmy guy, was gone for the day, and then I asked if he was married or not, and he told me, "No, just a single guy.""

"He kept working this whole time, and was probably getting a little pissed at me that I kept talking, but he was nice and polite. But when he did tell me that he was just a single guy, that's when I kinda started making some moves on him."

"Moves on him! What'd ya mean?"

"Oh some of it was just the way I was talking and some of the stuff I was saying, and yeah, I was kinda showing off my body to him a little. Flexed my arms a couple of times, like I needed to stretch or something, and of course I did grab my own crotch once to kinda of, "get it all adjusted and feel more comfortable," and of course I made damn sure I did that right when he was facing me! Once when he was facing me, I kinda, of all by accident, flexed my pecs a time or two just to see what he'd do, and I swear man, I do — he licked his lips! I know damn well that if anybody asked him if he did or not, he'd swear that he didn't, but believe me — his tongue came out — slid around his lips for a second, and then went back in. That is what I call, licking your lips! I mentioned how nice his arms looked, asked if he'd been working out at some gym someplace, and then as I slipped up behind him while he was leaning in and had his head under the hood, I just slipped up behind him, put a hand down on the truck — one on each side of him — kinda just let my body push up against him, leaned in close to his left ear and just said, "I know big Officer Jack and big Officer Bill! I'm Kenny — glad to meet you!"

"Oh shit man, you're kidding right — you are kidding me?"

"No Jack, no! No, I'm not! I was leaning there letting my crotch — which by this time was like a stiff broom handle, but I hope a lot thicker, just rub up against Troy's ass, and I know damn well he could feel it rubbing back there, and he tried to look back at me and then ask, "What man, what? Jack and Bill!? You're Kenny, the Officer Kenny? The officer they told me about?"

"I looked at him, kinda licked the side of his neck and said, 'Yeah man, yeah! That officer!'"

"He didn't say a fucking thing! All he did was wipe his hands real quickly, and then reached back and gave me one hell of a tight crotch grab! Damn it felt good! I reached up and grabbed a tit in each hand, of course had to feel 'em through his shirt, but none the less grabbed onto both of 'em, and then he took his other hand, reached around to his back side, and then grabbed onto my dick and my balls with both hands! All I could hear then was him saying, saying in a very nice soft tone, 'Oh shit man — oh shit! Pinch me man, pinch me! Oh shit, never expected this, in here today! Oh man — love it — I love it!'"

"I pulled my hands back, real quickly unbuckled my belt and unbuttoned my Levi's, and suggested that he put his hands down inside of my Levi's. I jokingly told him that his hands just might be a little cold, and they might need to get stuck someplace nice and hot, and kinda get warmed up some! He found out real quickly that he had ahold of one excited man, that had one very excited dick, on him! Man alive, his hands on my dick and my balls felt so fucking good! I know it was kinda of a struggle because of the position he was in and the way he was reaching around back, but he managed to get one of his hands down and under my bag, and roll my balls around some. Damn, I thought I had died and gone to heaven! Shit that felt so fucking good when he did that!"

"I unbuckled Troy's belt, unbuttoned the top of his pants, reached down inside and started handling his dick like it was a loaf of bread needing some kneading. And man, it rose! God it felt good! It got fucking harder and harder — right away! I know damn well that he was already hard before I even put my hands around him! I could kinda see it, and he made damn sure he did not move back away from the side of that truck! While he was working on the truck, he was trying to hide it, and at that same time, I was getting all good and excited in just trying to get him to get harder and harder!"

"For more than five minutes we stood there by the truck, feeling each other, licking each other's necks, pinching each other's tits and of course, grabbing and playing with the dick and balls on each other!"

"Troy kept looking toward the front of the shop, fearing that somebody could un-expectedly come walking in. He was really liking what was going on, but still kinda afraid that somebody might happen in and see us rubbing each other's dicks and grabbing each other's balls."

Looking at Kenny even a little more sternly, Jack suggested that maybe they ought to leave the station and maybe go for a cup of coffee someplace, 'a little more private,' so that nobody else heard the conversation, because he was very interested to know just what had happened and what had gone on.

Both of the officers left the station, since neither man was on-duty. They took advantage of being able to move to a little bit more of a private spot. In a corner booth of the neighborhood coffee shop, Jack then asked, "OK man, what happened then? Give it to me — I gotta hear this!"

"Well, standing there, just as close up to each other as two guys can get, I just giggled my crotch up against his ass and each of us grabbing dick and balls as much as we could, I told him I heard he was pretty good in bed, and then I told him that I wanted to see what this was really like, as I lowered my hands down and grabbed his crotch again and did the same to him, as he was doing to me. He kept trying to look toward the front of the shop. I know he was concerned that maybe somebody might be coming in and even though we were in the back. I know he was afraid that someone could come walking in and neither on of us hear them. So anyway, he finally said, 'Hey guy, this is shocking the hell out of me — making me horny as hell too, but let me turn around so I can see if anybody comes in the front. Okay?" I let him turn around, and as he did, then I saw him take a very good look at my face, and also all the way down my body! When he looked down, he really did just stop and stare at my crotch and lick his lips again! I could tell my crotch was making him hot as hell!! I rather guess maybe he hadn't really checked me out as much as he wanted to, before he finally found out just who I was. He thought I was just a normal customer, well — maybe one that was dressed for some gay parade, but nonetheless, just a normal customer. That was until, I leaned up against his butt and put both hands around him, and leaned forward onto him and his hot butt!"

"Kenny, Kenny, Kenny — I can not believe this," Jack kinda uttered as he grinned and rather shook his head back and forth. So, and then —?"

"Troy stood there, looked me over, up and down, then said, well from what I've been told about you so far, kinda looks like they weren't lying! Turn around man, turn around! I've been told about that ass you've got, and even though I can't see it right now — the way I wanna see it — let me see if it looks as fucking hot as Jack and Bill say it is!"

"As I turned, and then kinda bent over just ever so slightly, he told me, 'Yes, damn yes! They are right!' Then he said, 'Kenny, let me finish up on your truck, and then I hope you've got time to let me see that ass and that crotch both — up real close and real personal like — OK? You gonna have time to go over to my place for a little while?'"

"I looked at him and said, 'Hell yes man, hell yes! That's the only reason I needed to have my truck lubed today! I've been told about you and I decided that since I now, know how to find you — I wanted to see for myself! You're gonna let me fuck you, and maybe you're gonna fuck me too, right?'"

"He looked back at me, turned me around and rather jokingly looked at my ass again and then said, 'Hell yes man, hell yes! Let me finish putting some oil in this hunk of a truck that my new hunk of a cop is driving, and then let me close up the shop — maybe a little early, but I don't think maybe half an hour is gonna be too bad — then off to my place, and me into your ass! Right?"

"I looked at him and said, hell yes man, hell yes! You've got time for that I guess? You can do that?"

"He answered, 'Hell yes man, hell yes! To get into that hot ass, I'd make some changes of what I had to do, if necessary!'"

"He finished the truck, he closed up shop, and we headed over to his place! Now, I also know where his apartment is! And I'm gonna be visiting there a lot — well anyway I hope I am!"

"So Kenny, what happened when you got to his place? What happened?"

"Well, I guess maybe at first there was a lot of small talk about what I had been told about him, and what he had been told about me. He told me all about that first night out in Cemetery Park and how he had never done a guy before that, and of course he went into detail about how you, he, and Bill ended up doing a three way before you had to leave, and then he laid there and got fucked by Bill. He told me that he found out that night that he already knew Bill's boy Scotty, but he hasn't told Bill yet that he and Scotty are now fucking each other."

"What!? Wait!? Kenny, what did you just say!? Did you just say that Troy and Scotty are now fucking each other?"

"Yeah, yeah! Didn't you know that? I figured you knew that!"

"No, I didn't know that! When did this happen? How long has this been going on? No, I did not know this!"

"Well, I guess kinda just within the last week or so. That Scotty guy saw Troy in a gay bar one night, then found out where he owned a repair shop, and then went past there, and after they talked some, they went home and fucked each other. I guess Scotty now knows that Bill was one of the original guys playing with Troy, but I don't know if Scotty has told his Dad that he knows. Troy didn't say if Scotty has told Bill that yet or not."

"Oh shit man, I did not know any of this was going on. I haven't talked to Troy for a little more than a week, so I guess he and

Scotty got together after I last talked to Troy. Guess maybe I need to give him a call and see what's up."

"Yeah, Troy did tell me that he lets you and Bill call him, or stop by the shop, he doesn't call you guys for fear that maybe the wrong person will wonder just who was on the phone. So yeah, I'd give him a call. Besides I know he wants to do some more fucking around with you. He told me that he'd fuck with you every day if he could. He had some pretty good descriptions about that body of yours and the way you fuck a guy's ass, and of course he loves knowing that he's got all of that dick of yours, down in his throat! He likes the sex with you man, he does! Once he started talking about you, all he wanted to talk about was that enormous dick of yours! He told me that he really does have trouble understanding how a guy like him, can get so fucking exciting about some oversized big dick like — as he calls it — 'that enormous, oversized, big, thick, black, bull dick,' of yours! He said that he thought some guy — a guy new to getting fucked in the ass, should be afraid of something like that for a while, but he admits, he wants it every morning he wakes up. Jack, he loves that dick of yours!"

"Oh shit man — wait — wait! I'm still shocked over the Scotty thing! Damn! So Scotty is a gay guy — which I never knew, and his Dad does not know that either, but yet Scotty now knows that his Dad was one of the first guys fucking Troy, but Bill does not know that he knows that yet! Right? Oh shit! Damn man! Shit, you think I ought to tell Bill about Scott? Kenny, what do you think I should do? Oh man, what should I do? Any suggestions?"

"Yeah! Yeah, I think maybe you ought to just keep this to yourself, at least until you talk to Troy to see what he and Scotty said. Don't you?"

"Yeah, I guess so Kenny, I guess so! Man, who in the hell is gonna be the one to let Bill know that his boy is gay — is fucking guys — getting fucked by other guys, and also let him know that Scotty already knows that his own Dad, was the very first guy to fuck Troy? Oh Kenny, how are we gonna handle this?"

"Hey man, my first guess or suggestion would be to do a get together, maybe you, me, Troy, Bill and also Scotty and just let things work themselves out! Agree?"

"Yeah Kenny, yeah! I do. Gotta think this thing through. Never been in a situation where I needed to help some fuck buddy find out that his own son is gay and fucking around, and then also help him find out that his playmate is also his son's playmate. Oh shit Kenny, I wonder if Scotty is wanting to play with his Dad or not? Did Troy say? Did he know?"

"Yeah, he told me that Scotty doesn't have any problems with his Dad being gay and playing around. Troy asked him if that bothered him, and he said no, he was more disappointed that he never knew about you! Then he said that he asked if you and his Dad do play around together all the time. Troy told him, I guess, and that he knew that you're anxious to do him. He told Scotty that you had told him, that if he ever got a chance to get into Scotty's pants, that Troy was supposed to get you involved. So anyway — it kinda sounds to me like we've got two guys here — two guys that have known each other for years — and that both of you guys are real hungry for the other guy — right?"

"Hell yes, I guess so! I've wanted to get in Scotty's pants ever since that day at the pool, and I swear to God that he was packing an Idaho potato in the crotch of those Speedos. Damn man, this whole thing does mean that the day of me sucking on that dick is not gonna be too far away! Now, just gotta get things all set up so I can do it. Guess maybe I had better give Troy a call pretty damn quickly. I gotta get it set for me and that Scotty to get together, and then we gotta decide just how we're gonna let Bill know that his son gets fucked? Oh shit Kenny — maybe I should get together with Scotty, fuck him, let him fuck me, and then just tell Bill that we did it! Damn, that would be nasty! I can't to that until Bill knows about Scotty, right?"

"Yeah, yeah, I think maybe you're right. I don't think you ought to play around with Scotty until Bill knows either about Scotty being gay and playing around, or you just come out and tell Bill what is gonna happen. You know, we're gonna kinda need to find out if Bill is wanting to do his son, or maybe wanting his son to do him. Things could get kinda funny here if we don't handle this quite right."

"Right you are Kenny, right you are! But hey guy, that little bit of news for me kinda interrupted you telling me about what happened between you and Troy. Come on man, fill me in, let me know what happened and if you had fun with Troy."

"Oh hell yes man, hell yes! I had fun! We got over to his apartment, he offered me a Bud, which I of course accepted, and then he told me that since he'd been in the shop all day, he wanted to take a quick shower before we started, and I told him, OK, but that he was gonna have to make room for me in that shower too, cause I was gonna shower with him. Not that I really needed a shower right then, but I sure as hell was not gonna pass up on the opportunity of seeing him, and feeling him all over as soon as I could. He is one hell of a hot built guy! But then, I guess I don't need to tell you that! If it wasn't for you and Bill out there doing your supposedly hidden fucking around, none of us would be getting anything from Troy — big boy Troy."

"Jack, we got in that shower and I had my hands all over that guy! He's a big boy, and that shower stall was full. His 240 or so pounds, and my 225 made for a full stall! I reached down and cupped up right beneath his bag, and I thought maybe I had found a full bag of Christmas candy, or maybe I should say Christmas nuts. God man! He has got nice nuts! You sucked on those nuts any?"

"Oh yeah Kenny — oh yeah! Couple of times or so! Hell, come to think of it, it's now been more than just a couple of times. I agree, the first time I ate 'em, I was shocked! I gotta admit that the first couple of times that he and I did the ole man to man thing, he was so fucking taken with me, that everything we did, seemed to evolve all around me. Yeah, I admit, I'm a big man, and yeah, I've got a pretty big swonger on me, so all the talking and gasping was all aimed at me. But, you gotta also admit, he had never had a naked man in his hands like that before, and me being the big black guy, I guess that made it that much more exciting for me too. I was playing with a guy, built like a brick shit house, that was totally new to the game, so to say, so yeah, I was pretty damn well excited too! I found him and that football body of his exciting, but then, I gotta admit, that was not the first time for me to be man handling another guy and his rod and his ass — not to mention his nuts — but it sure as hell did turn me on too!"

"Hey guy! You and I have talked the man-to-man stuff, but we've never done it with each other. While we were in the fucking and sucking stage of doing each other, he was looking at my dick and making comments about how big mine is, and then he mentioned how one night you told Bill and him how big my dick is. He told me that obviously after you made some comments about my dick being as big as a black man's dick, he got all excited and knew he wanted it as soon as he could! But then — Troy told me you are damn well hung! Right? Do you carry the badge of honor for the black man, and support a really big piece of meat?"

Grinning broadly at Kenny, Jack came back with, "Hell yes man, hell yes!" Then looking more closely and directly at Kenny, Jack continued, "And unless you have got some big problem with it, you are just about to find out first hand. Come on, let's go over to Troy's, I wanna fuck that ass of yours! I've been watching that thing sway back and forth ever since you transferred over to our precinct, and I've gotten hard over it more than once, and I think it's time to poke it full with my, 'big, black, bull, officer's cock,' —as it's often referred to."

"Hey man — I sure as hell ain't gonna turn that kind of an offer down! I've been trying to see yours ever since that day in the restroom and you caught mine before I tucked it back in, but I've never seen yours, and yes, Jack, I've had a lot of big black men fucking my ass, and I sure as hell ain't gonna turn you and your rod down, but — what if Troy isn't home? I know we can't go to your place, but I doubt if my roommate is home at this time, so we could go over there."

"I wanna go over to Troy's in the hope that he'll be there too. You game if he's there?"

"Hell yeah man, hell yeah! You gonna call to see if he's there?"

"Yeah, yeah I will."

Jack called, found out Troy was home, and found out it was OK for the two of them to come by. In fact a little more than just OK! Troy was excited!

"Come on man, Troy is there and he is screaming with excitement that we are both coming over! He said he never expected this to happen! He is about ready to cum and we aren't even there yet! Come on!"

Chapter Ten

Lay Still and Get Ready!

Jack and Kenny showed up at my place about ten minutes after Jack called me, to see if I was home. When he asked me if it was OK for him and Kenny to come over for a little while, I was so fucking excited I damn near shit in my pants. I told him "Hell yes man, hell yes! Oh man alive, I sure as hell never expected this to happen today! Yeah guys, get over here right away!"

Jack and Kenny came in, I immediately gave Jack one hell of a major hug and crotch grab, and then the same thing to Kenny.

Kenny then looked at me and told me, "Well man! I told your big buddy here all about last night! I told him about you and me doing the old man on man thing and how much fucking fun you are. Course he then told me that he already knew that! He suggested that maybe you might not object to us coming over here and the three of us getting it on, so to say, especially since I've never had a chance to see just what he's hanging, and the way you talked about it last night, I really do wanna see it and use it!"

I looked at both of 'em, and told them that I was one hell of a lot more than glad that they came over, and I was anxious to do one hell of a lot more playing around with both of 'em.

Then looking at both of 'em, I added, "OK guys, I'm standing here with just a jock strap on, so start getting those clothes off and let's get things started. OK?"

And with that, Jack and Kenny headed for the bedroom, and I went into the kitchen and grabbed three Buds. I knew I'd never refuse a good cold one, and I knew both of my bedroom buddies, well enough, to know neither one of them would refuse one either, as long as they weren't on duty or scheduled to go on duty in a few hours.

I walked into the bedroom and I guess, rather to my surprise, Jack and Kenny were already getting to know each other, in a very close up and personal way. Kenny didn't even have his clothes off yet, but he sure did have his mouth full! Jack was standing in front of him, and with his hands on top of Kenny's head, and he was feeding him all of his big black dick!

"Well, Kenny my man," I rather asked as I came in the room, "I rather see that you did get that sausage stick into your mouth that you told me last night that you really were anxious for! How's it tasting man, taste good?"

Kenny looked over toward me, as much as possible, and shook his head, "Yeah."

Jack was standing there and very much enjoying the sucking of Kenny on his dick, and of course Kenny was in total heaven. Ten and a half or eleven inches of his co-officer's enormous dick now rammed down and into the back of his throat as far as it could go. Me, I was the one to figure out a way to get involved in all of this hot fun, and

I decided the chair was strong enough and sturdy enough for me to get up on it, and feed my dick into Jack's mouth and let him suck it dry. I wish I could have had a picture of the three of us! Me, standing up on a chair, feeding my dick into one of the hottest mouths in the state — my Officer Jack Tainer, and he feeding his dick into Officer Kenny Naughten's mouth! Poor Jack had to be looking and turned kinda sideways to get at my dick, and still feed his enormous rod into Kenny's mouth! This lasted for about four or five minutes until all of a sudden Kenny pulled off of Jack's dick, looked up and simply said, "I gotta get fucked by this thing, Jack you gotta fuck me!"

That rather changed everything. Not in a bad way, just a change.

"Jack I gotta get fucked by this enormous thing, man, I do!" Then looking over at me, Kenny continued, "Troy, you get fucked with this thing? He fucks you with this?"

Looking at Officer Kenny, as he laid down on the bed and was "ass anxious" for Jack to poke him a new asshole, I told him, "Yeah, hell yes man, hell yes! I told you last night about how fucking big that dick is, didn't I? Now you know for yourself! You're wanting that enormous thing up and in you aren't you? One look at that railroad tie and your ass just itches for it, don't it? Wouldn't you think that some guy — any guy that saw that thing would kinda decide it was too fucking big to take up in his ass? You know Kenny, I guess maybe, because he was one of the first guys that I had ever been handled by, maybe that was the reason I didn't get totally freaked out by just looking at it! Hell man, just seeing a man's big hard on stiff dick and having it in my hand, I guess that kinda kept me from thinking it was way too fucking big to put up in somebody's ass! I was fucking excited, and all I can remember now is, I wanted it, and I wanted it bad. After looking at it, it could have been a big black bathtub and I'd have told him to ram it up in me — I know I damn well would have! I was that fucking anxious and hungry to have that man in me, and on me, and using me for all it's worth! Now, guess what, it's gonna be going up in your ass! Lay still guy, you are gonna get it — all of it right up in there, in just about one minute! Lay still and get ready!"

Kenny laid there, Jack grabbed some Crisco, smeared it on his dick and some on Kenny's ass and climbed aboard! It only took about 15 seconds for Jack to reach down, slide his hand in between Kenny's thick muscular ass cheeks, slide them apart far enough to get his dick aimed for its target, and then go in!

"Oh shit! Oh damn!" Kenny rather let out, but not in a complaining or hurting manner, but actually in such as fashion that really did make me very jealous, that it was Kenny's hole getting it and not mine. Even without seeing his expression on his face, I could tell that Kenny was a little more than anxious and excited about getting Jack's beef stick pushed up and in his butt!

With jealously in my voice, and I know it was there, wanting it there or not, I asked him, "Feeling good? Kenny, how's it feeling?"

Turning his head over toward me and with one hell of a big smile on his face, he replied, "Oh shit man, this is fucking heaven! I have not felt this fucking good since the day ole man Sausserman bent me over and kissed my ass for the first time. That was the first time any person had spread my ass checks open and put his face right up in there and gave my old asshole a sweet little kiss. Seriously man, I've been kissed back there a lot since then, and I've had a lot of dicks back there too, but having this dick, going up in my ass and feeling as good as it does, yeah, it feels like that first time of getting my asshole kissed and sucked on by ole man Sausserman."

"Uhhh, who in the hell is ole man Sausserman? Who is that?" I asked as I watched Kenny getting the stick of meat up in his ass that I was so fucking anxious to feel going up in mine, but with patience, I knew that I was gonna get it yet before the night was out, and I'd be getting Kenny's again, too. "Kenny, who is ole man Sausserman?"

Laying there on his gut, and rather moaning to Jack to, "Do it man — do it — do it — fuck me man — fuck me." He then kind of giggled and said, "Oh he was just an ole guy we had on campus my sophomore year at North State. He was like a building manager, and he loved to come through the building, late at night, and find us guys walking the halls with nothing on. We all knew him and what he wanted, and anytime he found one of us, all bare assed, we ducked back into some hidden corner and either got a good blow job, or like that night with me, got one hell of a good ass kissing and sucking on! Hell man, I know some of us walked in the halls naked a lot more than necessary, just hoping that he'd be in the building and looking for some bare skin! Two and three o'clock in the morning, most of the guys that were still up were walking someplace, naked! Course, I'm sure some of 'em, me included, was getting some actions from some of the other dorm guys! I know I did as often as I could! I know some of the guys that probably never, any other time, ever did anything with another guy, let ole man Sausserman do stuff to them. He really wasn't that old — we just called him ole man, cause he was probably maybe 40, and hell, we were all like 19 and 20. So any man older than probably 30 or 35 was old to us. They were all like our old dads."

And with getting that out, Kenny let out a very big sigh and once again begged, "Oh Jack — oh do it man — do it — do it — fuck me man — fuck me." Then looking back at me again he softly added, "Oh Troy, this is so fucking good! Oh man, his dick up inside of me is heaven man, it is! Damn man I know now how you got fucked by this guy for your first fuck and can't stop yet! Oh man, I've never had a dick up inside of me that felt this fucking good! This thing is just filling me up! It is!"

I have to admit that his statement of how he had never had a dick up inside of himself that felt this good, was a little bit of a putdown since just about 20 or 21 hours ago, I had been up in there and he was begging me for more, more — but then, I had been fucked by Jack and that log before too, so I sure as hell did understand his feeling about how fucking good it felt. Only problem was, that was making me that much more anxious to get him out of the way, and let me get under Jack! I wanted that dick up in my ass, and I was getting pretty damned anxious for it!

Jack had been up and in Kenny's ass for probably about nine or ten minutes, and was using Kenny's hole as if he was driving a goal post into the ground, and without warning, he actually yelled, "Oh shit man — oh shit! Oh man — I'm cummmin man — I'm cummmmmmmin!!!"

I do have to admit, sitting there on the edge of the bed and watching that great big black man, with that enormously great big dick stuck in the ass end of Kenny, and watching how Jack's whole body just went into "steel stiff mode," was a little more than exciting. To watch such a man just turn almost into a marble statue as he strengthened every muscle in his body and turned every muscle in his body into a piece of stone when he shot off, was maybe even better than being under him, where I couldn't see how his massive body reacted to the climax that he let loose. Let loose in one hell of a big way! I actually sat there with my mouth kinda hanging open and I know my eyes wide open as I watched him move from one very, very, active mass of muscle to one very stoic and marble stoned mass of human muscle. Watching him and his actions, I all of a sudden understood how a man could have a fatal heart attack while in bed, having sex. Those deaths I know are most normally reported as, 'Died peacefully in his sleep.' Yeah right! Maybe peacefully, since he was getting a piece, but sure as hell, not in his sleep! All of a sudden, I wonder — do they ever report, "Died peacefully in HER sleep?"

"Oh shit Kenny, damn man, damn! What a fucking ass you have got man, what a fucking ass!" Jack managed to utter as he pulled all eleven inches of his manhood out of Kenny's ass and then rolled over beside him. "Damn man, should I say I just fucked one hot cop's ass? Or should I say — one hot ass — on a cop? Damn man — thanks — thanks!"

"You are welcome fellow officer, you are welcome! I will admit it, you are one of the city's finest! You are! Don't know just how we can declare that to get you a promotion, but I'm willing to put up posters and let the public know you are one good fucker! You OK now? You doing OK?"

Rather laughing at Kenny's stupid remarks, Jack answered, "Yeah man, yeah. I'm OK! But — gotta tell you, I didn't know I was on the campaign trail to get myself promoted! If that's what I'm up to, then I think I'd better be doing a hell of a lot more fucking at the station, and not hiding out doing it! Kenny, you're lucky. You and Troy here, both. You guys can live your true lives and don't have to play games so that nobody really knows the true you! Seriously men, seriously — the double life is a bitch, a real bitch!"

I looked over at Jack and replied, "I know that, I do. I gotta admit it was only for a few weeks that I kept lying to Shirley about why I couldn't come over that night, or why I had to go home early, but it was a bitch while I was doing it, it was!"

For just a few minutes we all three laid there, and I guess pondered what Jack had just said. Kinda quiet for three guys that were all there together to fuck the hell out of each other, but then, maybe, it was a needed rest period for the two that had just cut the forest down with all the sawing in and out, that had just gone on.

My ass was in need, and so I asked, "OK men, which one of you two city employees is gonna take care of this citizen of the city, and this person of need?"

Immediately Kenny said, "Me! I am! I just got the fucking hell fucked out of me, and so now it's my turn to pass it on! Come on man, give me that ass. I had it twice last night, and I get it again today! Give me your butt man — give me that tight football boy butt!"

Thank goodness I grabbed a little Crisco as I turned to lay down on the bed, because when Kenny said it was his turn to pass it on, he was not kidding. He poked me, he rammed me, he slammed me, he acted like a ragging elephant in my ass and within, not more, than three minutes, I was getting the strongest load of male cum that I had ever felt. The night before — from the same guy — with Bill — with Jack or one of the guys that I had brought home from the Cattle Barn, Kenny exploded in my ass bigger and stronger than any other time, that I had been loaded, so far! I thought Jack went into some unusual movements when he hit the load into Kenny, but I swear, I think that if I could have been watching what was going on, I honestly do think Kenny had a much bigger climax, than Jack did just a few minutes earlier!

All three of us were now totally exhausted, but not, to the point of no additional actions. Jack in me — me in Jack — me in Kenny, — Kenny in Jack, and at one time, both Kenny and Jack in me at the same time! My first double fuck, and when you have got two dicks the size of those two, up in your ass at the same time, it is an ass full, believe me!

When Kenny mentioned it, I honestly thought he was kidding, well that was until Jack got all excited about trying it, and trying it on me! He told me that he wanted me to know all of the tricks of the trade, so to say, about being in the gay lifestyle, and he knew that if I could take both his dick, and Kenny's, which was not hardly any smaller than Jack's was, but just a little shorter, and then I would be able to say, "Yes, I've done that!"

It took some convincing me, but when you have two big strong muscle built guys like Jack and Kenny encouraging you to do it, it's pretty damn hard to turn down. I finally agreed to try! I again emphasized to them, "Try." There was not one way in hell, that I was convinced that I was ever going to be able to get both of those cocks up in my ass, at the same time!

Surprise man! Do it! Honestly, do it! Whenever two men tell you that you need to be double fucked — do it! Felt fucking good!

Yes, I admit — I kept saying I could not do it — but I did! Yes, I did!

Jack laid down with his head up to toward the north, and Kenny laid down opposite, and then they intertwined their legs so that their crotches, their dicks and their bags were right up against each other's. With their dicks both pointing straight up in the air, they told me to get up above them, and then start squatting down on the tip of their dicks. Jack said that he'd hold 'em together so that when I came down, they'd both hit my asshole at the same time. And they did! Yes, they did! Yeah man, yeah, it was an asshole full, but shit man — what a tremendous feeling! I actually put both of their dicks up and in my ass, at the same time! Now I can say, "Yes, I've done that!" I not only got them up in there, I bounced up and down on them for probably two or three minutes, just getting the feeling of that much meat up and in my ass, all at once! Never turn an opportunity like that down, never! And yeah, for some funny reason while I had both of those dicks stuffed up in there and I was using both of 'em for all I could, all of a sudden I thought, "Hey man! I've got me a vanilla ice cream bar and a chocolate bar up in me at the same time!" I shook my head and wondered just why in the hell, would I think something like that, just because I was fucking lucky enough to get me a big white dick and a big black dick stuck up in there all at the same time? I was starting to wonder about my mind!

With everybody getting the dick of their choice, and of course me getting both of my dicks of choice — all at the same time — everybody had to admit that maybe the playtime for that night was over. Jack then suggested that they do some talking and deciding about just how we were gonna get Bill to find out about Scotty playing around, and also find out if Bill would want to get it on with Scotty or not. Planning, planning and decisions had to be made, before the wrong thing happened, and maybe Bill found out the wrong way! They decided, right way, wrong way, we had to do something so that we all knew that Bill knew about Scotty, and just who Scotty was playing around with!

Chapter Eleven

Looks Like a Four Way!

"Bill, I told you this was a long winding road back into here. It's well hidden and that's one of the reasons I wanna check it out and see just what's going on back here. Like I said earlier, tonight's just a look and see thing, but I couldn't come back here all by myself or guys would have known something was up."

Kenny wanted to go back into what is called, 'The Old Back Road' area, where he knew a lot of gay activities happened, and he asked Bill to come along so that he was not snooping around all alone, but rather had a "play partner" with him. Just a couple of gay guys, looking for a hiding place, to have some sex. He had told Bill to dress very casual, they were not going to be acting as policemen this time. And as I could attest to later, the casual was very casual, and damn hot as hell on both of 'em. Of course when you've got two policeman, both built like these two, you can expect some hot viewing when they are both dressed in tight, like I mean real tight, cut off shorts, baskets showing like part of a major theater showing, and no shirts! Just massive muscular arms, to die for! For two men that wanted to just blend in with the scenery — they really were — the scenery! A big part of it!

After quite a little drive back into some rather unattended spaces along the lake shore edge, they did drive past a couple of cars that were empty — meaning — somebody from those cars were out hiding someplace, and if of the normal type of visitors for this location, and especially at this time of night — gay guys, sucking and fucking — someplace in the bushes.

Kenny and Bill parked their car, well actually Kenny's F-150 after they had driven past an area that had about six empty cars parked, but nobody around any of them.

"Come on man," Kenny said to Bill. "Let's go for a little walk and see what he can find. If it's just guys fucking around with each other, I really don't care, my attitude is, let 'em fuck and suck, but if we find something that is not right, like an age thing or somebody being forced into something that we can tell is not right, then I'll need to make note of it for some later action. But tonight, it's just look and see, but remember, you and I are supposed to look like we are looking for some action too. If somebody comes onto you, tell him that yeah, you're interested but you and I wanna go do some fucking and sucking first, then you'll come back and find him, OK?"

"Yeah, yeah. This is turning out to be a little more exciting to me than I expected, when you asked me to come along tonight. Kenny, I've never been back in here before. Course, I couldn't come back in here with my uniform on, and so I guess I just kinda stayed with doing stuff back in town where I thought it was safer. You gay guys sure do know all of the good hideout spots don't you?"

Twice Kenny and Bill had to turn down some pretty major offers from some of the guys, that just all of a sudden came out of hiding in the bushes. When one man is fucking his partner, and then all of a sudden he pulls out so that he can go talk to two, 'major built body gods,' that is saying some pretty good stuff for the 'undercover cops,'' or in this case — the very exposed cops.

"Kenny, I gotta tell you man, never, never have I ever been in a situation like this, to where some horny guy, just all of a sudden appears, and straight out, tells me that he wants to fuck me and get fucked by me and my partner. Damn hot man, damn hot!"

"Hey Bill, that's the gay life! Especially back in some hidden spot like this spot. You can expect about anything to go on back here — hey Bill, look! Look up in front! Looks like a four way! Yeah man, look, it is! Hard to see, but yeah, it's four guys all together! Looks like three white guys and a black man. Come on, let's get closer. I wanna see this, I wanna see what they're up to."

As they walked forward quietly, Kenny leaned over toward Bill and said, "Bill look! Bill that's Troy and somebody. That's Troy!"

And with that, I looked over from fucking my buddy Danny in the ass and said, "Hi guys! Been expecting you. Meet my buddy Danny here! He's a little too tied up right not to get up and shake hands, but anyway, this is Danny."

Bill stood there in complete shock, but not near so, as when Jack, turned and said, "Hi guys! Been waiting for you!"

He was in the middle of a major fuck too, but his partner couldn't really be seen, since his face was down, and besides with Jack's big body, it pretty well hid the guy anyway! Besides with Jack's dark skin, he did not show up real brightly anyway!

Kenny was silent. Bill was shocked. He managed, "Uhhh Jack! Uhhh Troy! What in the hell is going on here guys? You guys bring your partners out here to fuck around with? Troy, why here? You got your own place you can use!"

Then looking at Jack, he kinda managed to ask, "Jack, who you got? Who you fucking man — who you got?"

Then to the total shock of the night, Scotty turned his head and said, "Me Dad — me! He's fucking me — your son!"

Kenny and Jack each looked at Bill to catch the reaction! Bill stood there motionless.

"Scotty!? Scotty, is that really you? Scotty, you're getting fucked!? Scotty, no I can't believe this, no! No! Looking at Kenny, he asked, "That can't be Scotty, is it!?

Kenny looked at Bill with a very serious expression and replied, "Yes Bill — yes! That is Scotty laying there and getting it in the ass! Did you not know that Scotty did the gay thing?"

"No, hell no I did not!" Then looking more at Scotty, Bill asked, "How long? How long you been doing this man? —How long you been doing this? Scotty, when did you start paying with guys like this — how long?"

Still laying on the ground, with Jack's long rod still stuck up in his ass — yes — laying there, getting one of the biggest dicks poked up in his ass as he's talking to his Dad about how long he's been getting fucked, Scotty looked at his Dad and said, "Ever since that late night when I saw you and that patrolman Shawn guy, sucking on each other in the car! I figured out right then, that if you could do that, and it could be that much fun, then I was gonna do it too! Dad, just because there were no lights on in my bedroom that night, did not mean I couldn't see out of my bedroom window and into the car down below, even though it was in the middle of the night. I had been wondering all night why you weren't home yet! Then I found out! I could see everything right through the windshield! Turned me on like crazy! There's gay bars in this town Dad, and even though I wasn't old enough to go in and buy a beer, you gotta be 21 in this stupid state to buy a beer, but I sure was old enough to stand outside and watch for some hunk of a guy that looked interesting to me. Hell man, when I was younger, I thought just going into a gay bar made a guy's dick get bigger, cause everyone of the guys that I eyeballed were showing big dicks and then thank goodness, letting me at 'em! Years Dad — years! I figured you knew about me a long time ago too, but I guess not! I thought you probably knew why I kept wanting to stay over at that Gene's house all the time. Hell man, other than sex, he and I didn't have anything in common! I guess us younger kids kind of know how to hide the finer things in life, better than the older ones do, don't we?"

Looking at Bill, Kenny finally asked, "Bill — Bill you OK with his?"

Kinda turning his head sideways some, and at the same time rather letting it drop ever so slightly, Bill finally said, "Yeah, yeah I guess so. I mean if his old man can do it, why shouldn't he? Yeah, yeah I guess so. Gotta admit, sure as hell took me back for a second or two, but yeah, I'm OK. Just gotta admit though that I think I should have been able to figure this out before this! I guess us parent types always think it's OK for us to do stuff, but not for the kids, even though they grow up too."

Then looking over toward Jack, Bill said, "I just gotta ask one thing right now though! Jack, how's his ass? He got a good ass? How's that ass feeling man, how's his ass? Better than his Dad's? Shit man — it's been probably two weeks now since I've had that tanker of a dick up in my ass, and what do I find here tonight — my son — laying there on the ground with the dick of death up in his ass, that I always kinda thought was just for me, slammed up in his ass and Jack all smiles about it!"

Continuing then, Bill did ask, "So Jack! Just how long you been doing me and my ass and my son's ass too? You sure as hell never told me you were fucking both of us, did you?"

"Hey Bill, this is the first time in this tight ass! Yes man, I admit, I've wanted this ass and also his dick for years now, but I didn't know he played around either! I just found out about two days ago when Troy told me he and Scotty were fucking each other! Shocked the hell out of me too!"

Then looking at me, Bill asked, "Oh! So you and Scotty have been fucking each other? Is that the reason you asked me that night in Cemetery Park if I'd seen Scotty's dick lately? Now I understand. You had to be fucking around with him back then, right?"

I had to set Bill straight, that like I had said that night in Cemetery Park, that was my very first time with a guy, but I remembered how fucking long Scotty's dick had gotten once he got a little older! I explained how Scotty had seen me in the Cattle Barn Bar and then tracked me down to the shop, and that was when we first did it together. I had to admit that yes, his son is one good fuck buddy to have around! And for a white guy, he sure does have one hell of a big stick!

"So Troy — just who in the hell are you fucking now man? Who you got tonight and where'd you find him?"

Looking up at Bill I answered, "Oh this is Danny — one of my drinking buddies from the Cattle Barn. Danny and I fuck around with each other quite a bit now, and since we needed a car that you wouldn't recognize when you guys got out here, we asked Danny if we could ride with him and use his car.

I had never been to this place before, face it man, I'm still new to the man on man thing, but since Jack told me about it and Kenny wanted to use it, then I asked Danny if he knew about it and he did. Once the idea came up about using this place, Danny really did want to be involved. Said he's had some of his best sex out here, and quite often with men that usually wear a uniform — if you understand what I mean!"

"Besides — Jack's got Scotty right now — I've got Danny right now, and Kenny's gonna have you in just about one minute, and so you can see — we needed to rather pair it all up. One man for each man, but yes — we do all know that before this night is over, everybody's gonna have to change partners — cause Scotty has already told us that he wants to finally — after years and years of wondering — wants to finally find out just what having sex with his old man is like! We may not be in Cemetery Park tonight, but just like in Cemetery Park, something new for the first time, is gonna happen here, tonight!"

About the Author

Wade Wright

Wade Wright is a semi-retired father of two daughters and four grandchildren. Transplanted many years ago from the state of Ohio, to the Southwest, now living alone — well with the exception of his Min Pin puppy, which has been his sole love for the past eight years! Enjoyed two gentlemen partnerships that each ended <u>way</u> before they were suppose to.

Wade Wright is also the author of *Yes, Cops Do It — Oh Yeah; The Two Straight Guys; Apartment 117* and also *Marshmallow Cream — and Hard Big Pieces of Chocolate,* available from The NazcaPlainsCorp.com, Amazon.com, or your local bookstore.

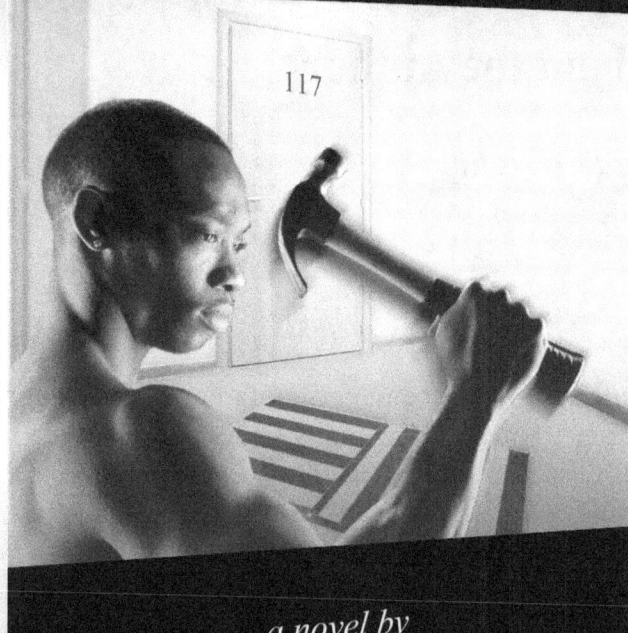

APARTMENT 117

a novel by

WADE WRIGHT

WRIGHT

APARTMENT 117

117

A BONER BOOK

The Two Straight Guys

Guys

A
BONER
BOOK

a novel by

Wade Wright

The Two Straight Guys

Wright

"YES, COPS DO IT, – OH YEAH!"

a collection of stories by

WADE WRIGHT

A BOXER BOOK

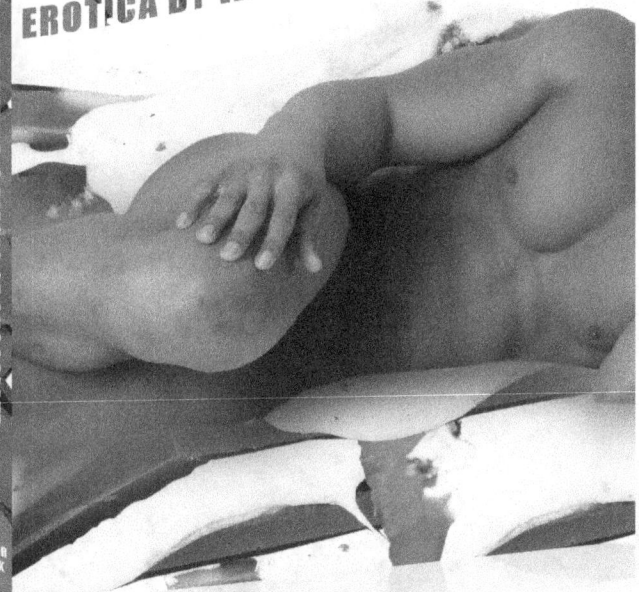

MARSHMALLOW CREAM
– AND HARD BIG PIECES OF CHOCOLATE

EROTICA BY WADE WRIGHT

A BONER BOOK

WRIGHT

MARSHMALLOW CREAM - AND HARD BIG PIECES OF CHOCOLATE

www.ingramcontent.com/pod-product-compliance
Lightning Source LLC
Chambersburg PA
CBHW051147260626
47170CB00005B/2003